W9-CNP-595

Odd Jobs

Odd Jobs

...

Patrick Delaney

© 2016 Patrick Delaney

All rights reserved.

ISBN: 1530708575
ISBN 13: 9781530708574

Introduction

...

PART-TIME AND VACATION JOBS TO earn spending money and help finance education were a shared experience of my generation. Jobs such as altar-boy work, for which small tips were paid, babysitting, house work, and lawn maintenance were begun in childhood and progressed to more complicated tasks through secondary school, college, graduate school, and beyond. This book describes the collective arc of jobs performed, from the carefree early work of our younger years to the more complicated employment undertaken later in life. The early jobs often convinced us to stay in school so that we wouldn't have to do laboring work for the rest of our lives. Ironically, those early jobs were often remembered fondly when we were faced with the rigors of work in the real world.

This is a book of fiction. The situations and characters portrayed here are not intended to depict actual events or people or to change in any way the fictional nature of the work. Any resemblance to actual persons and events is unintended and entirely coincidental.

Martin Waite

• • •

Serving the Cloth

· · ·

Martin Waite became aware of the reality of the Catholic Church in 1958 when Sister Flavia first fixed her fish-eyed gaze on him.

"Mr. Waite, I'm Sister Mary Flavia," she said. "Welcome to the eighth grade at Saint Jude's School—in the middle of the year." Her addition of the words "in the middle of the year" made it less a greeting and more a complaint about his interloping. He rose and extended his hand to her, but she retreated as if from a leper.

"I know you are not from Saint Paul," she said, "but where did you come from?"

Waite said, "I am from Saint Paul. I transferred from Edgecumbe School. My mom and dad wanted me to go to a Catholic school."

"That figures—you were in public school," Sister Flavia said. "And I'm assuming you are one more Irisher that we now have on our hands."

"If you're asking me if I am Irish, I am—one hundred percent. I'm the grandson of Jack Waite, a lawyer who was hung by the English for standing up against them for the rights of the Irish."

"Very impressive little speech. Now, baby Waite, sit down at the desk that has your name taped on its top."

Waite found his desk. It was odd to be called a baby at age thirteen and to have one's former school and heritage impugned by an adult.

Sister turned her attention to another student, who was seated near the cloak closet at the back of the classroom, noiselessly tracing circles on the blackboard. "Baby Swanson," she intoned, "stop wiping your filthy fingers on the blackboard."

Howard Swanson was a pathetic fellow who could just barely tie his own shoelaces. He was a student at Saint Jude's because his family lived within the parish boundaries and because, at age fifteen, he was still not ready for high school. His continued presence at Saint Jude's was the early Catholic version of affirmative action.

Swanson's family lived next to the Waite house on Oxford Avenue, and it became Waite's job to walk home with Howard every day. He despised the task at first as it often caused him to be late for basketball practice, but Waite came to like his role because of the touching gratitude the older boy showed him—not by saying anything, but by smiling shyly and waving his hand in a daily farewell salute.

The year passed under the sharp lash of Sister Flavia's tongue. When Waite's mother allowed him to have a party at his house with both boys and girls, he learned the truly perverse nature of the nun in charge of his education. The teenagers had played Spin the Bottle at his party, and somehow the story got out. On the Monday morning after that burlesque event, Sister called Waite to the front of the room and announced to the class that he would be going to hell. That was harsh stuff compared to Waite's hoped-for and milder consignment to purgatory, where hard time was done, but the punishment was not eternal.

In the same week as Waite's public damning, a good thing happened. Waite's cousin Dennis McCain and McCain's sidekick, George Ellman, were, for bad deportment, sent into Sister Flavia's class for behavioral formation. Sister knew both boys from previous school encounters and regarded them as criminal recidivists.

"Well," she said, "look what we have here: the overgrown infant and the stunted fool."

McCain, always the spokesman for the pair, beamed at her. "You know, Sister," he said, "if they don't want us in Sister Rose's class, we're happy to be with you again."

Sister Flavia moved quickly across the room, facing the newcomers. Without warning, she slapped Ellman with an open hand across the mouth. The big boy staggered, tripped over his partner's shoe, and fell on his back. McCain and Ellman laughed—loudly enough to attract the attention of the school principal, Sister Vivian, who was patrolling the hallways. Sister Vivian ripped open the door and entered the room, scaring the hell out of everyone except McCain and Ellman, who could not stop laughing.

"What in the world is going on in here?" she shrieked. "Stop that hyena noise, you two."

McCain and Ellman were shown to their newly assigned desks at the back of the classroom near the cloak-closet entrance. The doorway framed the misbegotten figure of Swanson, who sat with his head down to stay under the field of potentially flying objects and to avoid becoming involved in that day's demonstration of Sister Flavia's dominion over her students—a posture that would become all too familiar in the remainder of a school year spent with his rambunctious new neighbors.

The explosive conduct of Sister Flavia continued. The peak of her distress came near the end of the school year when one of her most troublesome charges, Fred DeCalva, suddenly disappeared for a week, causing general unrest and whispered gossip among the students. DeCalva's unexplained absence worried Waite too.

At the early age of twelve, DeCalva had begun to physically mature, and he had quickly grown into a large, awkward boy. He had always been Waite's friend, but he had become increasingly distant over the past two years. Something had definitely changed. On some late nights, when Waite looked out his bedroom window, he caught sight of DeCalva aimlessly scouring the empty neighborhood streets on his bicycle.

When DeCalva returned from his unexplained five-day absence, he slid into the classroom and took his seat noiselessly. The smirk that was usually on his face had been replaced with a chastened look.

Later that day, all the seventh graders were marched—boys in one line, girls in another—next door to Saint Jude's Church for the sacrament of confession. DeCalva behaved in an unprecedented way. He did not try to break out of line and make his escape to the outside, nor did he talk or chew gum.

On their arrival, the students learned that the dreaded Monsignor Fleming was on duty in the confessional. Fleming was an old Irish priest who spoke English in a circuitous way that few of the parishioners could understand. Always and everywhere, he used the word "consequently." Additionally, he always promoted religious vocations, which apparently were, in his opinion, the epitome of what one could achieve in this life.

"God made the heavens and our earthly bodies," he would say, "and, consequently, our purpose here on earth is to have children and raise a family or, at our best, to enter a vocation of religious service."

The notion of entering the religious life had been unthinkable to Waite until it was mentioned repeatedly to him by one of the assistant pastors, Father Krauthammer. Father Krauthammer had supervised the boys who served on the altar during mass, and he had recruited Waite to join the group. Except for small tips they got from the families of deceased or marrying parishioners, the boys served without financial payment. Most of the boys thought Father Krauthammer was a phony, but the influence of the young priest on Waite was enormous—until an inexplicable incident occurred at Saint Jude's summer camp in Wisconsin, when Waite was changing into his bathing suit in his cabin, and Krauthammer snuck up behind him and cupped his bare buttocks. The touch startled Waite, and he spun, covering his groin with his hand, to see Krauthammer standing nude in front of him, grinning.

At the top of his lungs, Waite screamed, "Get out of here, you fat bastard!"

Father Krauthammer dressed hurriedly and left the room. Waite told one of the other assistant pastors about the incident, but he did not even consider telling anyone else, including his parents. Nothing further happened until Krauthammer suddenly departed from Saint Jude's; he was assigned to another parish.

In the confessional, Monsignor Fleming had the distressing habit of announcing his understanding of sins that were being confessed to him in a voice so loud that many penitents were moved to tears of embarrassment. Waite's most embarrassing moment was when he confessed his encounter with Father Krauthammer, but, on that occasion, the Monsignor had lowered his voice and, in a sad tone, said that it wasn't Waite's fault.

DeCalva entered the confessional when it was his turn. Although he was only fourteen, he had a low, guttural voice. Everyone in line tried hard to overhear his sins, but all they heard was the animallike rumble. After a short time, the rumble stopped, and a clap of noise issued from the box.

"You did what?" Monsignor Fleming howled. "You went to Chicago with a girl for illicit purposes? At the age of fourteen?" A short time later, the boy emerged from the confessional with a stricken look on his face.

It was eventually revealed that DeCalva had taken his father's car and had driven from Saint Paul to Chicago, where he spent a weekend in a motel with a junior-high girl. The trip was short, and, when he returned to Minnesota, DeCalva was sent back to the classroom of Sister Flavia, who never again spoke to him or otherwise recognized his presence on earth.

For his penance, Monsignor Fleming ordered DeCalva to walk from the Cathedral Church in Saint Paul to the Basilica Church in Minneapolis and back, a distance of thirty miles. DeCalva took the bus both ways.

Soon after that event, DeCalva moved with his family to Montrose, a small farming community in southern Minnesota. Years later, when Waite was in law school, he read about the death of Fred DeCalva from a threshing-machine accident during crop harvesting on a Montrose farm.

Waite drove to Montrose to attend the visitation and funeral service. In the reception line at the wake, Fred's dad shook Waite's hand and then drew Waite aside. With tears in his eyes and in a confidential tone, he said, "Freddie was never the same after that son-of-a-bitch priest—Krauthammer or whatever his name was—molested him back in grade school. I should have spoken up at the time, but you know what the church was then. Our whole family would have been crushed."

Travels with Emmett

. . .

MARTIN WAITE AND HIS YOUNGER brother, Mickey, did after-school delivery work at Dermott's Appliances. At lunchtime on Martin's first day at the store, Emmett shared his sandwich with him and showed him the latest in a very long line of mechanical household devices he had invented. Emmett said that his Top-Juice machine would extract the essence of any fruit or vegetable. It was a strange-looking unit with a metal basket at the top, a long, crane-like neck, and a catch basin at the bottom. As Martin watched, Emmett inserted a peeled orange into the basket and pulled down on the curved neck, squeezing the orange and catching in the basin the pulpy orange juice that hadn't squirted into their faces.

"See, Martin? Most juicers lose upward of twenty-three percent of the juice in the process of pulverizing the fruit. Top-Juice loses almost none," Emmett said, cleaning his glasses as he spoke.

"How do you know that twenty-three percent or more is normally lost?" Waite asked. It was an unkind question that he regretted asking, given that it was clear that no one could actually know that information—and that, in the demonstration, Emmett's contraption had lost almost all of the juice of the orange.

"I heard that that figure was in Consumer Reports last year."

This was Emmett's scientific research method: not reading but referencing secondhand remarks that someone had made to him, which he repeated with a patina of authenticity.

Jim Dermott, the owner of the store, relied on his brother Emmett to run the service department in addition to performing his sales duties. Service tasks were a waste of the time of this surpassingly talented salesman, but Emmett was valuable in that role because service work brought him into contact with most of the customers of Dermott's. Emmett could persuade store customers that faulty operation of goods they bought at Dermott's was somehow to be expected and would be quickly fixed. In reality, items that came into the service department generally remained there for months. So the service customers got involved with the store for a long time and came to know Emmett in fixing their faulty goods; this would normally generate frustration and ill will on the part of a customer, but, in this case, it allowed them to know Emmett as an engaging and good-humored person. They often bought new and unrelated appliances from Emmett while their goods awaited completion of the repairs.

In Waite's time of employment at Dermott's, he grew used to seeing customers appear at the service window, an oval-shaped space cut into the wall like the reception window in a dental office, which opened into the large service department room where Emmett reigned. The place was littered with disassembled refrigerators and bulky parts. There Emmett could be found, often on his knees, thrashing through the astonishing mess on the floor of his domain with a look of concern on his face as he searched for appliances in repair.

When an elderly customer poked her face through the service window to ask for attention, Emmett would shoot up from the floor. His red face would materialize in the window in front of the startled person, his voice exploding into the customer's face: "Yes! What can I do for you?" If the customer didn't faint from the blast of Emmett's voice, she would be in for a long and confusing discussion.

In addition to running the service department, Emmett supervised the delivery truck on which the Waite brothers worked with a wizened veteran of the Dermott wars, Ray Wheelwright. Ray couldn't read—a sad affliction for a person to suffer as late as the 1960s—so when new or repaired goods were to be delivered to a customer, Emmett would sketch driving directions on Ray's arms with a grease pen. In a voice as thin as dusk, Ray always objected to this use of his skin as writing parchment, but his protests had no effect on Emmett. Prior to a delivery run, Ray's final admonition to Emmett was always the same: "If you're gonna write street directions on my arm, write them clear this time, Em, so that we don't get lost."

Martin and Mickey Waite consulted Emmett's scrawling on Ray's arms as they drove through the streets of Saint Paul looking for houses awaiting deliveries from Dermott's. Even when they were legible, Emmett's skin-quest directions were rarely accurate. Among other things, they usually failed to account for generational change. Ray's arms often directed them to locations that had long since been abandoned and to streets that had been rerouted or rededicated to other uses and closed to vehicular traffic. The result was that they frequently found themselves on delivery missions thought by Emmett to be nearby but that were actually at distant, newly numbered addresses.

On those trips that did conclude at their intended destinations, Martin and Mickey Waite would carry one end of a boxed appliance, and Ray would carry the other, often up tube-like back stairs in venues that were once large single-family dwellings but whose bedrooms and drawing parlors had become apartments in bastardized versions of their former residential glory. On those trips, the boys routinely stopped and talked with each other about school and girlfriends or anything other than the box they were carrying. During those interludes, it was easy for them to forget that they were carrying a hundred-pound appliance. So, without a thought about Ray, they sometimes released their end until they heard a faint, reedy protest.

"Come on, you shit birds," Ray would wheeze, still holding up the weighty and lengthy box from his end. The brothers would then collapse in laughter, leaving Ray holding the box until they collected themselves enough to take up their end and finish the delivery.

As soon as the delivery contingent returned to the store, Emmett would cross-examine Ray.

"Where in hell have you been with my nephews, Ray?" he would ask, laughing.

In answer, Ray would point to the faulty directions written on his arms. Emmett understood Ray's point without further discussion. It was clear that Emmett had once again sent them out on a wasted errand, and he would click his tongue in feigned self-disgust. Simultaneously, he shot a bemused half smile toward Martin and Mickey—a familiar look from Emmett that bespoke his joyful nature and his attitude that many things were problems but that they were all still lucky to be players on the grand stage of life at Dermott's.

The last time Martin and Mickey Waite saw their Uncle Emmett, he had been diminished by lung cancer. His son pushed him in a wheelchair down a long sidewalk to join the family-reunion party at a cousin's expansive lake property outside Minneapolis. From a distance, Emmett seemed to float toward them like a feather curling in the wind. An intravenous line ran from a bag suspended on a steel arm rising from his wheelchair. As he drew near, his five siblings and their children and grandchildren sang "When Irish Eyes Are Smiling." Emmett lifted his right arm as if in a bishop's blessing. The assembled family raised a cheer.

Emmett had never been publicly honored before that day.

Legal Education

. . .

Martin Waite started law school full of notions that would cause him many disillusioned moments. His vision going in was that he would be taught at a modern version of the Lyceum in ancient Greece—where the professors would discuss the philosophic and social implications of legislation and legal cases. He had heard of the case method of legal teaching but didn't know what it was. It had never occurred to him that no one would tell the freshman law students what a law student was supposed to learn—or that they wouldn't find out until about halfway through the second year of a three-year program.

On the first day of class, Waite sat in a room in which more than a hundred students were seated, stadium-style, at numbered places assigned on a chart taped to the classroom door. At exactly nine o'clock, the hour set for the torts class, a sleek young man in a gray three-piece suit strode into the room. He wrote a name on the blackboard—Professor Clement—and mounted the pedagogue's platform to stand behind a podium.

"I am," he said, "Professor Edward Clement. You may call me Professor Clement. I am a lawyer, though not an attorney. I am a graduate of the Columbia Law School and a past editor-in-chief of the *Columbia Law Review*." One of the students near Waite scoffed aloud at this recitation.

"Mr. Laughlin, are you somehow amused?" Professor Clement asked after consulting his seating chart. His tone was cold, and the question was stated in a manner designed to deter Laughlin from again volunteering anything in class and to convey the disdain and irrelevance with which Clement viewed the student's outburst and, for that matter, Mr. Laughlin himself.

Professor Clement surveyed the classroom for a sign of life. "Is there another of you who sees humor in this situation that you wish to express?" he asked in a faux-kindly voice. Hearing nothing, the professor continued with what Waite assumed would be a lengthy set of remarks about the students' entry into the study of law.

No such luck. Instead the professor said, "I will call on students from my picture graph as I see fit. Unless called upon, any student wishing to speak must raise his hand. Now, let us begin to examine the subject. Mr. Waite, can you tell us the holding in the case of *Birkmose v. Barker*?" he asked, looking directly at Waite. "I don't know what *Birkmose v. Barker* is," he said.

"It is the name of the case that I assigned for your reading by posting a notice on the bulletin board outside the dean's office. Did you fail to read it, Mr...uh...Waite?" the professor said, looking at his seating chart again.

Waite had no idea what the professor was talking about, and so he was mute.

"Mr. Waite, you're not in Kansas, or wherever you come from, anymore. You obviously did not do the reading assigned for today. Don't fail to do so again unless you wish to be in the roughly one-third of the class that flunks out after freshman year at this school. Can anyone answer the question? If not, this class will be over," said the professor, sliding his notes and the seating chart into his briefcase.

A lone hand shot up in the rear of the classroom.

"Yes, Miss—or Mrs.—Zachariason?" Professor Clement said with a bemused look on his face.

"I'm Ms. Zachariason. The holding of *Birkmose v. Barker*, Professor, is that if your dog is left unchained and bites a neighbor, you're liable for damages."

"Suppose your dog never bit anyone before, Miss Zachariason? Are you still liable? Or suppose you had the dog on a leash, and he broke loose and bit someone. Or, suppose you have a cat rather than a dog, and the cat bit someone."

The professor beamed at Ms. Zachariason, apparently pleased that she hadn't responded. Professor Clement and all the other students were surprised when Ms. Zachariason spoke again.

"Why all the hypotheticals, Professor? This was a dog, not a cat, who was known by the owner to be vicious and who was not adequately tied up."

"So the holding depends on the fact that the dog was vicious—is that what you're now telling us?"

"And the owner knew he was vicious—that is what I'm telling you," said Ms. Zachariason.

"So the dog was male. Suppose it were a bitch?" Professor Clement said, emphasizing the word "bitch."

"I'm through with this, Professor," said Ms. Zachariason.

"You might be indeed," said the professor, again folding papers into his briefcase. "The class is over."

When the mystique of law school began to wear off, Waite joined the clinical trial practice program and learned what were to become his most important legal lessons. On the day of his first clinic assignment, he sat before the bar in the lawyers' row at the front of the basement arraignment courtroom in Saint Paul, called "the Hole." The old Saint Paul courthouse had the look of a World War I military building—worn marble and wood that were so dry that the grain had begun to mummify. Judge Thomas "TNT" Spring was on the bench. The judge looked unhappy, as if he had sat on a bolt. Waite's client, Sweetwater Jones, had not shown up for the first call of cases, and the second and final call was imminent.

The Hole opened up to the street outside. It was a steamy, humid September morning. Judge Spring's arraignment calendar was suddenly interrupted by momentous barking and the burlesque sound of a car horn.

Sweetwater Jones entered the courtroom with two women in sequined disco dresses. He was dressed in style: high-heel boots, thin flared pants, and a feathered headpiece.

Waite rushed to the rear of the courtroom to intercept his client. As he did, the bailiff announced, "The last recall matter on the calendar, Your Honor: *State against Lamont Jones*."

Sweetwater's face beamed at the sound of his own name. He greeted Waite in a voice as loud as a race caller at a horse track. "Good morning, son," he shouted. "Where in hell is your boss?"

"I'll be representing you today," Waite said in a hushed tone.

"Like hell you will; I want the man."

"Look," Waite whispered, "this is just where you plead not guilty. Don't worry. Mr. Havisher will handle your case."

Judge Spring imbedded his gavel in the bench. "Counsel, please approach the bench with your client."

They walked up the aisle toward the bench, Sweetwater moving like a parade float. The clerk read the charge. "Lamont Jones, you are charged with possession of a firearm in violation of parole. What is your plea?"

Waite began, "Your Honor, the defendant pleads not guilty and requests—"

"Your Judge," Sweetwater interrupted, "this is prime bullshit."

Waite reentered the fray. "Your Honor, my client is not used to the courtroom and apologizes for his rude behavior."

Titters and a few laughs came from the spectators' benches.

"Well, you know, you see, Your Honor Judge," said Sweetwater, "I was holding the piece for a business associate. I was not possessin' it."

The spectators erupted in laughter.

"All right," the Judge exploded. "This is not a fact hearing; it is an arraignment. Defendant's plea of not guilty is entered. Bail is set at five thousand dollars. Adjourned."

The gavel pounded, and the bail bondsman, Weinberg, materialized at Rose's elbow. At the same time, a scream shot from the outside doorway to the courtroom.

"Get this dog off of me," shouted the sheriff's deputy who had been posted at the door.

Sweetwater's sequined ladies shrieked with laughter. "Hey, Sweet Man," one of them yelled from the back, "Avis got the sheriff down on the ground. He's gonna bite off his privatcies."

Waite worked out the cost of a bail bond with Weinberg and snuck out the side door into the court officers' hallway.

The Homeowners

· · ·

MARTIN AND NANCY WAITE PURCHASED their first home after they had a baby and ran out of room in their apartment.

They bought the house directly from the seller without the involvement of a realtor. At the closing meeting, the seller, Claude Singer, smiled and declared in his broad Texan accent, "You kids are gonna love it here!"

On December 28, they moved their few pieces of furniture into the place. The house was of the type realtors usually referred to as a starter, and it was all they could afford. Although Nancy came from a wealthy San Francisco family, her parents had cut her off when she met and married Martin. And Martin didn't get paid very much as he was a young lawyer and just starting out.

The temperature was five degrees Fahrenheit in Minneapolis. The flat roof over the family room in the back of the Waites' new house was laden with at least a foot of recently fallen snow. Under its shingles was a major ice dam, which, as the roof warmed from the heat of the house, melted and created a pool of water that resulted in a leaky roof. A few days after moving into the house, the ice dam that had melted and collected around the wrought iron chandelier above the family room spewed rusty water onto their baby, Jonathan, as he crawled across the family room on the one good piece of floor covering they had—an old Persian rug given to them by Nancy's aunt.

Martin, who was completely ignorant of leaky roofs and home maintenance in general, phoned Singer at the forwarding number he had produced at the closing and explained that the house he just sold them had a leaky roof that had to be fixed. Claude Singer laughed and said something about the damned Minnesota winters making the "buyer beware" principle truly important.

"Where are you now, Mr. Singer?"

"I'm in the new, dry house of my brother-in-law. Why do you want to know where I am?"

"Because I'll have a process guy serve you with a summons and complaint. You should tell me where you are and when you would like to be served so that he doesn't surprise you when you are in a restaurant or taking a shower or whatever."

"I'll be gone, Marty. But get up on the roof, and shovel the snow. The opportunity for self-help is one reason you're gonna love it in that house."

That was the Waites' last contact with Claude Singer.

When the snow melted in the spring—some of it into their house—they got several cost estimates for having the house reroofed.

The roofing estimates ranged from about eight thousand to twelve thousand dollars—until they got a bid from Dennis Horvath, a roofer who had replaced the roof of one of Marty's senior legal colleagues and had apparently done a good job. Martin and Nancy asked Horvath to come over and give them an estimate. He agreed to do that and said he would be there the next evening about five thirty. Dennis missed that appointment and a succeeding appointment he made with the Waites.

After the second missed appointment, Marty called Dennis's home phone that night. The roofer answered abruptly, "Yeah, this is Horvath."

"Mr. Horvath," said Marty, "This is Martin Waite. I hope you are still interested in giving us a reroofing estimate. Remember? 4201 York Avenue?"

"Who the hell is this?" Dennis demanded.

"Martin Waite calling you, Mr. Horvath. You've missed two appointments we made with you to come to our house to give us a roofing estimate."

"Well, shit. I drove over to Saint Paul three different times to talk to you, and I couldn't find your house. Couldn't even find a York Avenue."

Waite said, "We're in Minneapolis, as I believe I told you. Maybe that's why you couldn't find our place."

"No kidding?" Horvath said, laughing and coughing. "OK. I'll be over tonight at six o'clock, but I will have to bring my three kids with me. The old lady took off for South Dakota to visit her sick mother. Let's hope she stays there."

"We'll be home waiting for you," said Waite, thinking he'd never see the guy.

At six thirty, Marty and Nancy sat out on their front steps with their baby. A 1957 Dodge panel truck pulled around the corner, narrowly missing a tree. A radiator was roped onto the old vehicle as a front bumper. Horvath stepped out of the truck and stumbled across the street to where they were sitting.

"You folks know where I can find 4201 York?" he asked, pulling a cigarette out of his jean top and lighting up.

As Waite stood to welcome the roofer and tell him he was at 4201 York, he was struck by how short and hunched the man was. He looked like an ape that had just leaped from a tree: short stature, long arms, oversized hands, and rheumy eyes.

Martin held out his hand and said, "We are glad you are here, Mr. Horvath. I'm Martin, and this is my wife, Nancy Waite."

"Looks like about a twenty-five-hundred-dollar job to me," said Horvath, without shaking hands. "But I'll give it a closer look." The Waites gave each other a hopeful glance. Twenty-five hundred dollars was much lower than they expected to hear from any bidder.

By then, Horvath's kids had tumbled out of their dad's truck: one boy, about fourteen, who Horvath introduced as Cade; a second boy, Elder, who Horvath said was seven or eight; and finally a three-year-old, who was Jim.

"Cute boys, Mr. Horvath," said Nancy, who got the finger from Cade for that remark.

"You have any ladders?" asked Dennis.

"Yeah, there's one in the garage, "said Marty, "but I assume you have your own ladders that are long enough to reach the roof peaks."

"Sure, I've got ladders, but they are on another jobsite right now. Let me see what you got. It'll probably be enough for me to give you an estimate."

They got one of Waite's ladders out of the garage, and Dennis scrambled up to take a look at the side roof.

"Looks bad," exclaimed Horvath. "Let me look at that flat back roof you mentioned."

They moved the ladder to the back of the house to get access to the roof above the family room. Horvath and, to the discomfort of the Waites, his son Cade climbed up and stood fifteen feet above the backyard looking at the nearly flat roof.

"Christ, what a mess," Dennis shouted down to Martin. "Do you land helicopters up here, or what?" Then he repeated his estimate. "We'll do the roof for twenty-five hundred dollars." The neighbors working in their gardens turned in the direction of the loud voice.

"Deal," said Waite.

Dennis Horvath said he could start in two weeks, and he'd be completed in two more weeks or sooner. Martin said he'd like to check out his reference with Tom Claridge, the fellow lawyer who had employed Dennis on a job and who had recommended him to Waite—just to make sure about the quality of Dennis's work.

The two men stood on the front lawn, sizing each other up, Waite looking down and the diminutive Dennis staring up defiantly.

Dennis said, "That's just insulting, Waite. If you can't trust me on quality, I mean, what the hell?"

"I don't know you from Mickey Rooney," said Martin, at once sorry that he made the comparison to a little person.

"Lawyers. Shit!" Dennis said. "Go ahead and call Casey, but my bid offer will only be open for the next week. Be sure to get back to me."

In the meantime, Nancy was inside the house supplying cookies and milk to the three Horvath boys. The boys were staring at Jonathan. Each of them wanted to kiss the baby, including the fourteen-year-old Cade. She didn't let them touch their lips to her little angel, but she was surprised and impressed with them that they wanted to do so. Nancy didn't know that in the future, when Dennis was on the job, she would end up babysitting those boys and would learn to like them less and less as time went on.

The deal was made and a written agreement was drafted providing for a full reroofing of the Waite house in two weeks' time by the Dennis Horvath Roof Raisers for a bid contract price of twenty-five hundred dollars. Dennis claimed he would do the work alone, with occasional help from his children. The idea that this little weasel could complete the roof work in two weeks was a dubious proposition in Martin's view, and he assumed Dennis's reference to having his children help was only a joke.

Under the contract, work was to begin on June 10. By June 16, the Waites were restive, wondering why their man had not shown up to begin work and why he hadn't returned their phone calls. After a few more days, at about seven o'clock in the morning, Nancy and Marty awoke to the sound of a clatter on their roof, a noise that turned out to be the current shingles being shoveled off the roof. Martin tore outside and beheld Dennis and Cade standing athwart the high peak of the roof, laughing and shoveling the old shingles off the roof directly onto the hedge of bushes surrounding the front of the house.

Waite shielded his eyes against the rising sun and yelled, "Dennis, what are you doing? It's all landing on the bushes and crushing them."

A piercing cackle issued from the rooftop as though the practice of his trade had set free the evil that surely must have possessed Horvath. "I'll be right down," he yelled to Waite. Then he picked his son up from behind with a bear hug and pretended that he was going to launch him off the roof.

Waite shouted in panic: "Put that kid down, Dennis; you might drop him."

Dennis and Cade let out shouts of laughter that shattered the morning quiet. Martin could only wonder what he had let himself in for by getting involved with such a wild man.

On the second day on the job, all three Horvath kids came over. Nancy made them lunch and an afternoon snack. At one point during the afternoon, as she tried to get Jonathon to sleep, she looked out a side window and saw Dennis, followed too closely by Cade, going up the ladder to the side of the high, slanting part of the roof. She saw Dennis stop quickly and kick in midair down toward his son as if he were trying to knock him off the ladder. Dennis howled joyfully. She ran over to the window, raised it, and shouted out to Dennis. "Don't bother your son while he is going up that ladder, Dennis. You might knock him off."

"Mind your own damn business, Missus," Dennis said. He always called Nancy "Missus."

"You watch how you talk to me, Dennis," she said. "Marty will be home in a short time and knock you down a peg or two."

When Martin returned from work, he told Dennis that he didn't want the Horvath kids, including Cade, up on his roof. He said he had no insurance to cover child workers. That admonition was followed by what the Waites assumed was a retaliatory move on the part of Dennis: absenting himself from the job for two full weeks. After the third day that he failed to show up, Marty called the phone number that Dennis had given them and got Mrs. Horvath on the phone, freshly returned from South Dakota.

"I don't know where Dennis is," she said. "The guys at the bar—Big Al's—said that he talked about going to Alaska to fish. I hope you didn't give him an advance on the job he's doing for you. Did you?"

"Yeah, the contract called for five hundred dollars in advance, so I gave it to him," said Marty.

"Dumb shit," was all she said.

When Dennis returned to the job, he did so without the kids, and he appeared humbled. He asked Marty to come outside and confer with him.

"Now look," he said, "I know I screwed up. I went fishing for a few days with two guys from Al's, and I spent all the money you gave me. Could you advance me another five hundred dollars so that I can buy some food for the wife and kids?"

"You took off for Alaska during the middle of our job?"

"Not Alaska," Dennis said, "Annandale—just west of town."

Martin looked at him and shook his head in doubt and disappointment. "OK. I'll give you another five hundred dollars to keep you going, but you have to be over here every day for as long as it takes you to finish."

Dennis looked up at Martin with the beginnings of a tear in his eye. "I'll get her done, Mr. Waite. Don't worry," he said, gloving the five-hundred-dollar check from Marty and heading for his car. "I'll see you tomorrow."

Late that night, at two thirty in the morning, Martin got a call from a Hennepin County Sheriff's deputy at the downtown Minneapolis jail, who said they had a sorry-looking guy in a cell on a charge of driving under the influence. "Dennis Horvath. Says he's your employee. He's a regular down here."

Martin shook his head. He asked the deputy to tell Mr. Horvath that he'd be down in a while. He threw on a pair of khakis and a golf shirt, emerged into the steaming hot July night, and got into his car, arriving at the jail in about twenty-five minutes. He went directly to the front desk of the holding tank, identified himself, and asked to have Dennis Horvath released to his recognizance.

The jailer came out and said, "You want Horvath released to you, Mr. Waite? I don't know why you would want to take a chance on that slug, but you can have him if you want him. You realize that by having him released to you, you are telling the court that you'll make sure he'll be here for his first appearance?"

"Yeah, I get it," said Martin, though this was his first personal recognizance, and he didn't fully understand it.

"All right. I'll let him out of the holding cell, and you can haul him out of here."

Within a few minutes, Martin saw Dennis walking down the hallway ahead of the jailer, looking bleary eyed.

Martin spoke to him right away. "OK, Dennis. I don't know why I'm doing this, but you are being released on my personal recognizance. That means you don't have to buy a bail bond, but I'm personally responsible for your showing up for your first hearing. You'd better remember that, and do not cross me. Do you understand me?"

Dennis lifted his eyes and looked at Martin. "Who the hell are you, anyway?" he asked.

"Who am I?" Martin exploded. "I'm your current employer on a reroofing job, and right now I'm your ticket out of here."

"Well, let's get going. I got to call my old lady and get her to come down here so that we can drive the truck home."

The booking deputy said that the truck had been towed to the city lot. Martin put a hand on Dennis's shoulder. "I'll drive you home, and you can take care of the truck tomorrow."

As they walked out the door of the huge county building, Dennis again asked Martin who he was.

Back at the Waites' house, Dennis actually showed up every day for six days in a row, without his kids, and he progressed toward finishing the job. On the day before he was to complete the work, Martin asked him if he had obtained lien waivers, the standard form to absolve the homeowner of liability to any of Dennis's suppliers to guard against their claiming that they hadn't been paid and making a claim against the property.

Dennis looked at him and announced, "Mr. Waite, this damn house will never lean."

Martin gave him lien-waiver forms and told him to get them signed by any and all subcontractors and material suppliers. Horvath said all he had was one shingle-and-paint supplier: the local hardware store.

So, the following day, after inspecting the jobsite to the extent that he could from the ground, and having accepted Horvath's apology for crushing the hedge around the house with shingles cast off the roof, Martin paid Dennis the remainder of the contract price, obtained the paint supplier's lien waiver, and invited Dennis in for a beer.

Dennis spoke in his customary blasting tone, even though they were only a few feet apart at the kitchen table. "Mr. Waite, you're a good guy, but that wife of yours is really a bitch," he said.

"What in the world are you talking about?" said Martin. "Nancy told me that she made lunch for you and your kids, that she watched after your kids, and that she brought you cold bottles of beer during the days to keep you from getting too hot up there on the roof."

"Yeah, I guess," Dennis said, downing the rest of his bottle of beer and rising to leave. "I just hope my car starts so that I can get out of here."

As he departed, Waite heard the Horvath car backfire and scrape down the street dragging a broken tailpipe.

Impressing the In-Laws

. . .

WAITE WAS TIRED OF LEGAL work and looked forward to leaving for a vacation with Nancy. Their plan was to go first to San Francisco to see her parents and from there to go to Cabo San Lucas for a long stretch in the sun. He and Nancy had been married for fifteen years, and they had traveled out to see her parents only twice during that time. This sort of sudden departure from work in the middle of the most important and complicated case he had ever handled was perfect "Marty Waite, trial lawyer."

"How long will you be gone?" his associate asked.

"Until our money runs out," said Waite, "or two weeks from Saturday, whichever comes sooner."

"I assume you will have your computer and cell phone with you while you're gone so that we will be able to get you when we need to."

Waite told him that he would be hard to reach.

The home of Nancy Waite's parents was in the Pacific Heights area of San Francisco. When they reached the place, the afternoon sun had settled on the bay. Waite felt his stomach shift into neutral. The haze above the bay had dissolved. Below, on the water, there was a circus of color and movement: sailboats gliding toward the far reach in the Friday night regatta, sailing boats coming under the Bay

Bridge, big commercial boats, and hot-air balloons descending from the heavens to float over the bridge on their way to a lower pass over the waves—silent but for the occasional breathy exhalations of the fire-heated air needed to maintain altitude.

The drive up to the house passed a lengthy and straight row of cypress trees on one side. On the other side was a still pond of water where swans circled lazily. A wooden rowboat was pulled up on the bank of the pond, a boat in which Waite imagined that many proposals had been made and considered.

At the beginning of a circular driveway, the white wooden expanse of a house with several screen porches and verandas could be seen as if in the eye of a camera filming the summer home of a president. They approached the house. Through a large front window, Waite observed a white-jacketed butler inside carrying a tray.

Nancy's parents were out for dinner, so Waite would not see them right away. The last time he saw them was on an earlier trip to their winter house in Palm Springs. They didn't like him a bit: his job as a trial lawyer, his serious pursuit of Nancy, his whole act. But they had tried to be pleasant, especially Mrs. Plato, a woman who seemed to be interested in people and a bit careful about the direction of their conversation, steering it to social events. Nancy's father, Henry, was out of it. He looked like the rich uncle on the Monopoly board, an overlapping white mustache hiding his teeth. He might have lost his way in a golf event in the late 1940s and shown up forty years later for his next shot.

Aunt Martha Ringway was home to greet the Waites, and Martin talked with her about law, politics, and religion. Martha observed that Waite's representation of criminal defendants must have been "inconvenient." Waite tried to picture Martha in the company of some of his flamboyant criminal clients. She would probably take their conduct in court as plays produced for her amusement.

After a time with Martha, Waite began to admire her estranged and, in that sense, rosy view of life. Things she loathed were labeled "OK, I suppose." Unpleasant facts were dismissed as "not worthy of discussion."

On the subject of Waite's heritage, Aunt Martha asked, "Is Waite an English name?"

Martin said, no; he was Irish. At that, Martha tilted her head as if she had found a dead mouse in a kitchen drawer.

"I like the Irish," said Martha. "We had an Irish girl, Kitty, who was the best nanny our children ever had."

That night, at the Olympic Club, there was a party attended by many of Nancy's San Francisco friends. Waite encountered a boring group of stuffed-up bankers. Still, the event was fun. In fact, Waite was the hit of the party, telling war stories about his seedier cases. He drank rum and tonics with abandon. Nancy left him at the party at midnight and arranged for him to get a ride home with someone named Rogers Horn. Before she left, Nancy whispered to Waite that she would be in the first bedroom to the left at the top of the stairs.

When Horn dropped him off at the front door, Waite wore the apprehension of someone with severely disabled senses and coordination. He expected a huge dog to charge around the side of the house and jump him. He fumbled for a key and then remembered he had none. He tried the doorknob; thank God, the front door was open. Inside, the hall light was on, allowing him to find his shoelaces. He took his shoes off and left them at the bottom of the stairs. Mincing upstairs, at one point he tipped dangerously backward and righted himself with a balance-beam motion of his arms. He turned right at the top of the stairs, carefully rotated the knob of the bedroom door, and stepped lightly into the room. Luckily, the bathroom light was on. Waite slid into the room, doffed his clothes in a pile, and stepped into the glass-enclosed shower. He turned on a hot spray of water and soaped up heavily. The thought of surprising Nancy in bed was a good prospect. He dried, rubbed his teeth with a forefinger coated with toothpaste, and moved out of the bathroom into the dark bedroom. The fresh air blowing through the curtain felt great on his naked body.

In a moment of boldness born of Bacardi, Waite quickly slipped under the covers behind what he took to be Nancy's slumbering form. A high-pitched squawking filled the room. Jesus Christ! He stared into the crazed eyes of the lady of the house, Nancy's mother! She regarded him with a mixture of terror and automatically asserted superiority.

"Martin," she said, "may I know what you are doing in Henry's and my bed?" A bedside lamp snapped on, and Nancy's father bolted upright. He snatched wire-frame glasses from his bed table and thrust them onto his face. He looked toward Martin, as if at a swimming snake from the perch of a canoe. Indeed, Waite looked like a swimmer, straining under the sheets to protect himself from the frenzied Mrs. Plato.

Henry Plato shook his head and said resignedly, "I knew something like this would happen with you, Waite."

The Manikowski Family

. . .

Delivering the Goods

· · ·

ON THE STARTING DAY OF his first job during college, Jerry Manikowski reported to a room in the back of the street-level store at Eighteenth and Nicollet in Minneapolis where the proprietor, Bud Johnson, was busy pressing dry-cleaned clothes on the mangle, a large, heavily padded device that clamped clothes between two opposing ironing pads. It spewed steam, filling the room with heated fog.

Bud shook Jerry's hand with a sweaty palm and told him to come into his small office, grab a chair, and sit down to have a beer.

"What courses are you taking at the university," Bud asked Jerry.

"Classes for what I hope will turn out to be a money-manager job."

"You are planning to be a stock broker?" Bud asked, squinting at him as if he had just divulged an intention to rob a bank.

"Yeah, that's my present plan."

"They're criminals, you know. Maybe not while they're in school, but pretty much all of them become crooks after they're in the business." Bud said this with an air of certainty that didn't seem to auger well for their future as employer-employee. Then he laughed and said he was just kidding; he didn't even know any stockbrokers.

"All right, kid," Bud said, "let's talk about important things. Do you know how to play cards?"

"I know a little gin rummy. Picked it up at the fraternity house."

Bud pulled a deck of cards out of his shirt pocket. He shuffled them quickly and gave them the fan flourish that practiced card players perform, a sort of bending that arches the cards up and fires them down into a deck.

"OK. We'll play three streets to two hundred and fifty points, at a tenth of a cent a point. How's that?" asked Bud, smiling.

"What do you mean by 'three streets'?" asked Jerry.

"Three games at once. See. Look here on the score sheet. There are three headings for each player. You are J, until I think of a better name. And I'm Ace, the name I always have in cards. So, in the first hand, let's say I have gin and you are left with twenty-five points in your hand. Under my name—Ace—we write fifty, twenty-five for my gin and twenty-five for your points. On the next hand, let's say I go down for five points, and you have ten unmelded points in your hand. My five is deducted from your ten, giving me five points. We add those five points to my total of fifty points scored by me in the first game, and add five in the second Ace column, giving me a total of sixty points in the first street and five in the second street. Then we move on to the next hand. And so on. Do you get it?"

"You mean we're playing Hollywood. Is that right?"

"So you are a gin player."

Jerry said, "Not really. I'm just learning. Like, what did you mean when you said you went down for? What's 'going down'?"

"You're joking, right? I mean that if the down card is five and, after you discard, you can meld your cards without having five or more unmelded points, you lay them down. If I can't play all my unmelded cards on your hand, you subtract my unplayable points, say sixteen, and you get sixteen points minus whatever melded cards you laid down. That is what's called "going down." The trick is to go down as quickly as you can, leaving your opponent with a lot of unmelded points in his hand. Do you get what I mean?"

"Sort of," said Jerry. "But the way we play it at the fraternity is that you have to make gin to score points."

"Well, you fraternity boys don't know sic 'em. Let's play the right way. We'll keep a running tab of what you owe me at a tenth of a cent a point. And by the end of the year, if you haven't crashed my truck and you're still working here, you'll owe me plenty. Maybe fifty thousand dollars or more," Bud said, laughing.

"Maybe you'll owe money."

"Dream on, Hortense. OK. You've had your first card lesson from me. Now, let's load up some clean clothes, and I'll show you how to take them out in the truck and deliver them."

Bud took him into the revolving hanger room where the dry-cleaned and pressed clothes were arranged in alphabetical order. He covered them with plastic bags and attached invoices showing the contents and the names and addresses where they were to be delivered.

The clothing for the following run was hung on an adjoining rack and arranged in the order of the route to be taken by the delivery truck.

Bud told Jerry to transfer the piles of the cleaned clothing in order onto the rack in the Johnson panel truck behind the shop. Together they loaded ten or twenty to-be-delivered bunches of clothes and then got into the truck. Bud backed up, drove down the alley, turned on Sixteenth, and shot into the rush-hour traffic on Nicollet Avenue, changing lanes three times within the first two blocks and honking his horn and flashing the bird at car and truck drivers on all sides. Without warning, as they neared the corner of Nicollet and Thirty-First Street, Bud swerved across to the right, and came to a screeching stop in front of Homer's Bar.

He hopped out of the truck and said, "All right, Gin Wiz, let's go in here and get ourselves a little toner before we set out on our route."

They strolled into the bar and took two stools. The bartender said, "Well, if it isn't the savior of the haberdashery business right here at our little place again. Welcome, Mr. Johnson, and to your young friend. What can I serve you gents?"

"I'll tell you what, Homer. We'll have two glasses of schnapps," said Bud. "One for me and one for my new delivery man, Jerry here—if he's got the balls for it."

Jerry started to protest that he had just had a beer and that he really wasn't interested in any hard stuff, let alone schnapps, at this time of day.

Bud quieted him with a pat on the shoulder. "Don't worry, Jerry. I pay for this round, and we move on to our work. You will please do me the favor of joining me for an afternoon touch of class: pure German schnapps—always good for your temperament and your stomach."

"To our new partnership," Bud said, raising his glass in a toast and then downing its blinding-hot contents in one swallow.

After Jerry had one sip of schnapps, they left and set out on their route, delivering mostly to the big houses around Lake of the Isles and then up the hill into the Kenwood neighborhood.

Jerry learned the dry-cleaning delivery business with a heavy dose of instruction from Bud, an always entertaining and usually half-snapped instructor.

One day in November, Bud sent him down to the Rothschild building in downtown Minneapolis to deliver a month's worth of shirts, slacks, and dress clothes to one of the true characters in town, the trial lawyer Sam Wormsley, a thrice-divorced and always-well-dressed son of the famous founder of the Wormsley law firm, an old time Minneapolis institution started by Sam's father, Jim. When Jerry pulled into the Rothschild ramp to find a parking place, it was full. He drove around and up the floors until he spotted an open place on the second floor that was marked "For Deliveries."

As he approached and started to turn into the open spot, a raucous protest was set up by the blare of a car horn and the open-windowed screaming of the driver of a chrome-heavy Cadillac going the wrong way in the ramp but obviously destined for the same spot. The front of Jerry's panel truck and the Cadillac's snout stopped simultaneously at the threshold of the open space. Jerry looked over at the driver of the finned Caddy and recognized him as Ray Seal, the host of the local afternoon pop radio show of choice, a man who referred to himself on the air as the Wizard of the Wax, the Purveyor of the Platters, and the Deacon of the Disks.

Jerry's contestant for the open parking spot got out of the silver Cadillac and strode over to Jerry's panel truck like a plantation owner to a horse-drawn wagon.

"What do you want to do about this, son?" the tinted-blond Mr. Seal demanded in a loud voice. "If you had any gumption, you'd move that piece of junk so that I can park and make it to my radio show on time."

Jerry stepped out of the truck and approached him to talk. Seal backed up as he saw Jerry's height and strong, T-shirted arms. "Sir, I believe the sign here designates this spot for deliveries, which is what I am doing," said Jerry.

As they spoke, the attorney Sam Wormsley stepped into the parking lot and walked up to them. "Hello, Mr. Seal. What is the trouble here?"

"The trouble here is that this teenager driving his dry-cleaning truck doesn't seem to know who I am and is apparently having trouble seeing why he shouldn't move his tin can out of the way so that

I can park and make my radio show on time. Maybe you could clue him in."

Wormsley saw the "For Deliveries" sign and asked Jerry if he was making a delivery.

"Yes, I'm delivering dry-cleaning to a condominium in this building to someone named Samuel Wormsley."

"So, Pinky Boy," Wormsley said, directly to bill Seal, "you'd better back out of the way, or I'm going to give this young man my legal opinion that he has every right to beat your fat bag of a body. How's that?"

Seal huffed back to his Cadillac, got in, and sped up the ramp, laying rubber as he went. Sam Wormsley took Jerry across the street to Zelo's restaurant for a beer.

When Bill Seal called Johnson's Cleaners to complain about the behavior of its "delivery boy," as he referred to Jerry, Bud Johnson told him that if he ever saw him, he was going to tie him up, bring him down to his store, and send him around for a few cycles in one of his dry-cleaning machines.

Attendant

. . .

ONE SUMMER, JANICE MANIKOWSKI WAS asked by her college friend
Sarah Turlowe and Jane Turlowe, Sarah's sister, to serve as a bridesmaid for both of them in their weddings. The hysteria that accompa-
nies wedding planning was only heightened by the Turlowe sisters'
unfortunate choice to be married in a double ceremony.

Janice was hesitant about participating in the prewedding parties
because she had been out of the social scene for the prior two years,
which she had spent as a novice in a Benedictine convent. And in any
case, her nature had always been to be reticent in the world of people
and things, but she decided to attend.

Against her own better judgment but lacking someone to accom-
pany her, she took her mother's suggestion and brought her brother
Jerry as a sort of date to the first scheduled prewedding party. The
festivities started at a large house on Lake Minnetonka, from which
seventy guests were taken out for a cruise on the lake on a large pad-
dle boat. Elaborate hors d'oeuvres were on board, and music played
over speakers throughout the boat. Janice danced once with Jerry,
who was drinking liberal amounts of the vodka-spiked punch that
was being served out of two large silver bowls on the upper deck of
the boat. Janice couldn't take the punch, so she had two Cokes while
onboard.

Jerry was made more sociable by the punch he was pouring down. As the party proceeded, he became increasingly voluble, introducing himself around the vessel and boasting about his success as a securities broker whenever he could corner someone to listen to him on this topic, which was boring to most of the college-age partygoers. Later in the night, he had harsh words with two guys who had heard him bragging and told him to flake off. Jerry turned and threw a large cup of punch in the faces of the two antagonistic listeners. Some of the spillage made it down to the dark water, but a good deal of it blew in the fresh evening breeze onto the windows of the wheelhouse cabin.

Janice was present for this event, and she was mortified. She asked Jerry to please not embarrass her further, to which he loudly replied, "Look, Sister, I'm getting tired of the attitude of the college heroes in this group, so get over it." In a slightly lower voice, Jerry said, "I'm not thrilled about being here with my old-maid younger sister, but I came. Now the guests are unhappy with me about talking business, just because they don't understand it. But I'll try to be good until we dock and can go home." He hugged Janice, transferring a glob of shrimp sauce from his chin to her white dress.

What a way to reenter society, she thought.

As the day of the tandem weddings approached, Sarah Turlowe confided to Janice that her intended groom, Harry, had a serious case of cold feet and was talking about postponing the ceremony indefinitely. Sarah said she had told Harry that he simply could not upset the wedding by delaying the event and ruining things for them and for her sister.

Janice observed that if Harry was uncommitted to the marriage, there were probably more important things for Sarah to consider than upsetting the wedding arrangements.

"He's going through with it, Janice—whether he likes it or not," said the bride.

Janice said, "My advice to you is to not worry; just let things cool off for a while. All grooms get cold feet, don't they?"

"That's easy for you to say; you're not in danger of being left at the altar."

"You are right," said Janice. "I'm not in danger of being left at the altar. But there is a danger that I'll never get close to any man, let alone to a marriage altar."

"Oh, hell, you're nervous from doing your time in the convent. There will be plenty of love in your life."

"I think I've typecast myself as an old-maid do-gooder religious geek who will become an old maid permanently."

"For God's sake, you're two years out of college; that's hardly an old maid."

"Well, anyway," said Janice, "we were talking about your worries, not mine—about Harry's lack of resolve. I say trust his good sense. He's obviously crazy about you, and he doesn't want to lose you. He knows he's not going to back out. He'll settle down."

"Thanks, Janice," said Sarah, laying against Janice in an uncomfortably tight hug.

That night, at her mom's house, Janice sought some reassurance from her mother and her sister, Marcy, about the likelihood of the wedding going ahead.

She got little comfort from Marcy, who said, "What is that stooge Harry up to? The wedding is three weeks away. He's at the free-throw line. Now he has to shoot the ball."

Janice was annoyed with her sister's casual analysis of the situation through a seedy basketball analogy.

Their mother said, "Girls, let me tell you something. Men always get worried before they marry. They are like dogs, worried exclusively about two things: their next scrap of food and when their next encounter will occur with some sleazy cur who will meet their insatiable needs."

"Mom! How can you talk like that?"

"They're all the same. Men—male dogs. Your father was one."

This sent Janice to her room and her face into her pillow. In moments, she was asleep.

As the wedding drew near, Janice had to buy a pair of shoes to wear with her bridesmaid's dress. The stores she checked in town—the Golden Rule, Field-Schlick, Frank Murphy's—had no shoes in women's large sizes, let alone in the ballerina pair that went with the wedding outfit. Janice moaned to her mother about the unfairness of a woman having big feet, and her mother made the mistake of mentioning the matter to Janice's brother Jerry. The next day, Jerry relayed the story to Ron Swanson, a guy at his securities firm who had a quirky sense of humor and loved to play practical jokes that displayed what he thought of as his comic genius.

Swanson called Janice that night. "Hello, is this Miss Janice Manikowski, the bridesmaid?" he intoned in a winnowing, whiny voice.

"Yes, this is she," said Janice. "May I ask who is calling?"

"A friend, Miss Manikowski—Ron Swanson. I understand you may have some difficulty in shoe-size requirements and that you are looking for a certain slipper for an upcoming wedding. I'm calling to help. We here at Dayton's department store in Minneapolis have a wide variety of shoes of the type you are looking for."

"Do you have the Capezio Light Stepper model?" Janice asked.

"Yes, indeed we do, Miss Manikowski. What size shoe do you wear?"

"They are elevens, I'm sorry to say. Eleven and a half in some models."

Swanson shouted into the phone. "Elevens? Sometimes eleven and a half? Are you sure about your size?"

"Yes, I'm sure," Janice said defensively, her face reddening. "Don't you think I know my own shoe size?"

Swanson was unrelenting. "Well, there could be some mistake, I suppose. But let me say, Miss Manikowski, we sell shoes here, not canoes. You'd have to go to the navy surplus store for canoes."

"Well," said Janice, "you are a rude one. You need a lesson in respect, Mr. Swenson."

"Swanson," he said quickly.

Janice slammed down the phone receiver and pounded her foot on the linoleum kitchen floor, all to the great amusement of her sister and mom, who had gathered at the kitchen door to witness the commotion.

On the wedding day, Janice got dressed early in the morning and spent at least an hour nervously checking herself in the full mirror on her bedroom closet door. She slipped a pair of falsies into her bra to fill out the sagging bridesmaid's dress. She thought she looked like a farm wife ready for Sunday-go-to-meeting. When her friend and co-bridesmaid stopped in front of her house and beeped her car horn, she hurried out of the house and left for the wedding in a nervous state.

As the pastor of Savior Lutheran Church turned to greet the assembled wedding guests, Sarah Turlowe's fiancé, Harry, shifted in his chair on the altar in a way that seemed perceptibly nervous to those in the bridal party and even to some in the congregation. But things proceeded to that moment in the ceremony when the officiant turned to the couples and asked, first of Harry: "Do you, Harold Stockton, take this woman to be your lawful wife?"

Harry stared dumbly at the minister. "I really don't know, Pastor," he said, setting into motion some serious shifting in chairs and foot shuffling in the congregation.

"Well, Harry," said the minister," you probably should go into the sacristy and spend a moment thinking about this. I'll hear the vows of the other couple first."

With that admonition, Harry strode off the altar and into the anteroom at the side of the altar, leaving his bride-to-be with her head in her hands. The pastor proceeded with the rites of marriage of the other couple, keeping one eye cocked on the sacristy from which he expected Harry to appear momentarily. After the final "I dos" from Jane Turlowe and her new husband, the concerned minister walked back to check on the state of the undecided groom. Harry was gone.

The pastor reappeared on the altar and announced to the hushed congregation, "Ladies and gentlemen, it seems that one of the young men to be united in marriage today must have been taken ill and is no longer with us."

This was an unfortunate way to sum up the situation. The congregation, as if one person, gasped at the news that Harry was no longer with them. It was one of those circumstances where no remedial words were adequate. Sniffling, crying, and a few muffled groans of grief were heard in the church. The bride cried out loudly: "Harry." Harry's parents rushed up the middle aisle through the altar area to the sacristy, where they expected to find Harry's dead body.

The pastor tried to regain equilibrium. "Please," he shouted from the altar, "take hold of yourselves. This is apparently a case of a bridegroom who became nervous at the last moment and departed."

His words drifted away as he began to recognize that he had put into play an unfortunate chain of suppositions with his announcement that the bridegroom was no longer with them and had departed. The pastor considered reframing his explanation of the situation, but he decided his words would only further befuddle the wedding guests, who could be forgiven for their confusion, confronted as they were by one smiling married sister, clutching the arm of her new husband, while the other bride-to-have-been was slumped in a chair, disabled and crying, her head down on her knees.

After the proceedings, which had lasted almost as long as a Catholic wedding, the six wedding attendants floated down the center aisle, smiling as they turned their gazes from the brides' side to the grooms' side of the church. The stricken congregation—who had been taken from a joyous double wedding, through an announcement of what they took to be the death of one of the bridegrooms, to a statement that the missing groom had departed—numbly followed the attendants out of the church.

They ended up at a reception at the University Club. Janice made her way through the crowd, largely unnoticed, to step up to the bar and quickly drink the first three martinis of her life. In view of the events at the church, the reception was somber for everyone but Janice, who got potted and danced too closely with the successfully married groom, whom she called Harry, forgetting that Harry was the reluctant groom who had vanished from the scene. Later, she remembered nothing but the martinis.

At the end of the reception, Janice was led out the front door by Bunny something, one of her co-bridesmaids.

Outside, on the threshold of the club, she gave her head a shake to clear it and, in the process, launched both of her contact lenses out of her eyes and into the shrubs at the sides of the front stairs. Now she was a lost soul. Bunny had called ahead for a cab, which was waiting in the street. Bunny pushed Janice into the back seat and handed a note with Janice's address written on it to the driver.

The cab pulled away from the curb in a blast, as if leaving the starting line at a race course. Janice was thrown against the back seat, her arms splayed across the seat cushion. Quickly, and unexpectedly to Janice, the cab flew over the edge of Summit Hill, hurtling down the perilously pitched street at an impossible speed. After going a block down the steep incline, the taxi lost its footing and slid into a parked car, the cabbie shouting loudly enough at this misfortune to make Janice curl up in the fetal position and cry out, "Oh God."

Alarmed by the unprecedented appeal to God being uttered in his vehicle, the cabdriver yelled back to Janice in a tone that seemed to blame the accident on her: "Miss, settle down! I'll call an ambulance to get you the hell out of my car."

Within a few minutes, the sirens of an approaching emergency vehicle frightened Janice into enough mental clarity to reach down the front of her dress into her bra and snatch out her falsies so that they wouldn't be discovered in the emergency room where she was likely bound. She didn't know where to put the conical foam-rubber disks and finally stuffed them down into the space between the cushions in the back seat of the cab.

After a quick review by the attending physician at Saint Joseph's Hospital, who found that she had suffered no injury, Janice called home. Her mother could barely hear her; Janice was still drunk, sniffling and blowing her nose into her lace bridesmaid's hanky.

"What the heck happened to you, Janice? Did you drop the punch bowl onto your head?" her mother said with a snort.

"No, I'm fine. But you won't believe what happened. Sarah got stood up at the altar. Only her sister ended up getting married. I left the reception in a cab that got into an accident. But if you get me home and let me take a nap first, I'll sit down and explain the whole day to you and Marcy."

"What the hell?" her mother exclaimed. "OK. I'll come and get you."

That evening, after a two-hour nap, Janice gave Marcy and her mother a thorough account of the surpassingly awful day. They laughed on hearing Janice's tale, particularly when she tearfully revealed the humiliating secret that she had stuffed her falsies into the seat cushions of the cab.

The next day, her brother's friend, Ron Swanson, struck again with another telephone call.

"Hello," he said in a deep, disguised voice. "Am I speaking to Miss Janice Manikowski?"

"Yes. May I ask who is calling?" Janice said.

"Yes, ma'am. This is Sergeant Elmer Rusnacko from the Saint Paul Police Department. May I ask you, Miss Manikowski, are you of the Jewish persuasion?"

"No, I'm a Catholic. Why do you ask if I'm Jewish?"

"That was my guess—that you are a Polish Catholic—so I was surprised at what my officers found yesterday in a taxicab that got into an accident on Summit Hill. Perhaps I should begin by making sure first: Were you in a yellow cab that hit a parked car on Summit Hill yesterday at about three in the afternoon?"

"Yes, as a matter of fact I was, Sergeant. Why? Do you need me as a witness?"

"No, ma'am, no witness needed here. But I'm interested in knowing whether you left any personal articles in the taxi after the accident."

She was stunned. Her damn falsies! But she thought quickly and issued an outright denial of being the owner of anything that was missing. The sergeant went on: "We found two of those little Jewish beanies—yarmulkes I think they call them—stuffed into the seat cushion of the cab, and we wondered whether they belonged to you."

Janice's face went red, standing there alone in her own house. Finally, Ron could hold his laughter no longer.

"Just kidding, Janice," he sputtered out. "This is Ron Swanson, your brother Jerry's friend. He put me up to this."

"You should be ashamed of yourself, Mr. Swenson, or Swanson, or whatever your Scandahoovian name is. You can go straight to hell!" she screamed into the phone and slammed it down.

Janice dropped into a kitchen chair and asked her mother if she could have another martinez—or whatever they called those drinks—and then have a discussion with her about whether she should reconsider her decision to leave the nunhood.

Life's Peak Moment

. . .

MARCY MANIKOWSKI LANDED A SUMMER job at Saint Mary's Lodge in Glacier Park because her mother knew the Green family, who lived in Saint Paul and who operated the lodge in Montana during the warm months of the year. Mrs. Green said that Marcy could work in the dining room as a waitress even though she hadn't made timely application and was only nineteen, which was under the normal lower age limit of twenty for lodge employment. But when she arrived at the lodge to report for work, Mrs. Green recognized how pretty and how personable Marcy was, and she immediately concluded that she ought to work at the front desk.

"But I don't know anything about greeting hotel guests or handling a telephone switchboard," Marcy protested.

"Don't worry about experience," said Mrs. Green. "With those blue eyes and that smile, you are a natural for front-desk work. Grab your luggage, and we'll get you in a dorm room and then over to meet Iantha Thornberry. She supervises the front desk and sets the schedules of the people who work there."

She followed Mrs. Green down two flights of stairs, both of which were lined with windows to the outside, where one of the national park's highest and most jagged-peaked mountain ranges towered above the startling blue of Saint Mary's Lake. The sight of the lake and mountains transported her. It seemed as though she was descending a staircase in a celestial precinct, not part of any reality she had experienced. Just seeing them was thrilling, which was good because Marcy didn't know that her work hours would not allow her time to do much exploration of the mountains.

Mrs. Green and Marcy went across the road to one of the women's dorms where Marcy would be living in a room with two other first timers at the lodge, both college students at Carleton College in Northfield, Minnesota.

"Where do you go to school?" Mrs. Green asked Marcy.

"This fall I'll be a sophomore at Colorado University in Boulder."

"Good. We have several kids from Colorado here this year. You'll probably know some of them."

As they returned to the lodge, they approached the front desk. Mrs. Green introduced Marcy to her new boss, Iantha Thornberry, and then departed.

"Hello, Iantha," Marcy said.

"You may call me Miss Thornberry, or Ma'am, if that is more comfortable for you."

Miss Thornberry showed her around the desk area and the back office. "Now, we are not in need of any additional front-desk people, but I'll fit you in because Mrs. Green has ordered me to do it. Just remember that while you're working in this area you will answer to me. Now, let's look in the back office. We have a typewriter, a calculator, and a telex. I trust you know how to operate all this elementary equipment."

"Actually, the only one I know how to use is the typewriter."

"Have you taken business courses in school?" Ms. Thornberry asked in an antagonized voice.

"No. I am an English major in undergraduate school, and then I hope to be working on a master's in English."

"What are you going to do with that when you graduate?"

"I'll probably teach English, but that isn't the point," said Marcy, feeling that she was getting uncomfortably close to an argument with her new supervisor.

"Why isn't that the point?"

"Because higher education is an end in itself rather than a means to train for jobs. It's a way to learn how to learn throughout your lifetime."

"You sound like a college bulletin. I'll turn you into an effective office worker anyway, if you have any practical sense at all."

Within a week on the job, Marcy and Iantha found that they really did not like each other. Marcy was not good at clerical tasks, but she was great at meeting and greeting the hotel guests, a skill Iantha lacked and envied.

One day when Marcy was at the front desk, a couple approached and signed in as Mr. and Mrs. Parsons, Charles and Amanda, of Philadelphia. They said they wanted to stay in room 401 in the lodge.

Marcy said, "I'm sorry, we have guests staying in that room for four nights."

"Well, I trust you will be able to fit us in there, because we always stay in that room," Mr. Parsons said.

"I'll check, and we'll accommodate you in some way. But there are guests in room 401.

"Well, you should tell the Greens that you have to move those guests into a different room so that we can be where we want to be."

Marcy was put off by this imperious manner, and she ended the conversation quickly by telling Mr. Parsons that if he would wait she would call her boss to consult about the availability of 401 and get him a decision immediately. She stepped into the back office and called Mrs. Green on the intercom. Mrs. Green told her she would have to give the Parsons the room they wanted and find another for the guests who were booked into it at that moment, so Marcy was able to reappear promptly at the front desk to tell Mr. Parsons that she could give them 401.

He said, "Fine. Kindly give me the sign-in form and the keys so that we can go up to our room to rest." There was no thank-you from Mr. Parsons or even a smile acknowledging her success in securing the room they wanted. Marcy's encounter with the man left her feeling dreary.

After the Parsons had been at the lodge for two days of a planned week-long stay, he showed up at the desk in the early morning when both Marcy and Miss Thornberry were on duty.

"We trust everything is working out well in your stay with us, Mr. Parsons," Miss Thornberry chirped like a finch.

"Not really. Last night, when Mrs. Parsons and I were in our room having a cocktail, we heard some loud Indian noise out in the road in front of the lodge. It sounded sort of like drumming and singing. Miserable racket, I'd say."

"Well, as a longtime guest here," Miss Thornberry said, "you know that the Blackfeet put on a nightly show out by the ceremonial teepee in front of the lodge, and they play music. The show ends by eight o'clock to ensure quiet for the guests. But we're sorry you are unhappy. Is there anything else we can do for you?"

"Maybe you've had Indian music before, but I don't ever remember a noise as obnoxious as the drumming and caterwauling we heard last night. That really doesn't belong at a first-class hotel; do you think?"

Marcy could not restrain herself. She broke into the discussion.

"Mr. Parsons," she said calmly, "you have to remember that we're not in Philadelphia, and we all have to remember that this is Blackfoot tribal land where we now stand, and, indeed, that the whole of Glacier Park was theirs before we took it away."

"I'm not interested in an American history lesson from you, young lady. Please just tell the management that we don't want to hear that racket tonight after six o'clock." He turned and walked away.

Miss Thornberry glared as if Marcy had told the guest to go stuff himself.

"Listen," said Thorn, "you are not here to insult the guests but to make them content. Mr. and Mrs. Green will be unhappy to hear about this. I will make sure that Mr. Green particularly learns of your insolent behavior and that Mrs. Green hears of your inability to handle the front desk."

Marcy received a note summoning her to report to Mr. Green the next afternoon. She approached his office with trepidation and was ushered into his wood-paneled office, which had elk, moose, and buffalo heads mounted on the walls and Indian rugs spread on the floor and thrown over his leather couch and chairs.

"OK, Marcy Manikowski," Hance Green said, shifting his long, rough frame on the couch. "What makes you think you have any right to mistreat our guests? Our aim is to show our guests some hospitality. Do you know that Mr. Parsons is an efficiency expert we have in once a year to snoop around and give us a report on what he thinks of our hotel? So, you really took on the wrong guests."

She held back the tears that were building up as she beheld the older gentleman.

"I didn't really take him on, Mr. Green. He just made me mad saying that the Indian music was caterwauling, like the Blackfeet don't belong here."

Now Hance's blood rose. "Did that little twerp say the Indians don't belong here?"

"He didn't come right out and say they don't belong here, but that was his attitude. I told him that he was not in Philadelphia anymore."

"You told him that? Good for you!" Hance Green cried out, springing from the couch and laughing. "I'll send that goddamn

Eastern yahoo out of here today. And he'll see how long I can take to pay his phony efficiency-report bill."

"I'm sorry I caused this whole thing, Mr. Green," Marcy said.

"I'm glad you did. I like your style, and I'm going to tell old Thorn to give you the best hours at the front desk."

Early in the season, Marcy met the man of her dreams, Jim Stampler. He was a student at the University of Colorado and a summer bartender in the cocktail lounge adjacent to the main dining room of Saint Mary's Lodge. They liked each other right away. He called her M, and she called him Stamp. He brought her a screwdriver to drink at the front desk every day, which tasted good and she passed off to Thorn as orange juice that she needed for a vitamin C deficiency.

Stamp had been an army paratrooper before college, and he was on the Colorado State University football team. When they began their romance, Marcy had just turned nineteen, and Stamp was twenty-two, a much older man.

Before the three-month summer season had come to a close, Marcy agreed to drive Stamp out to Fort Collins, Colorado, to report for football practice.

"Do you think this heap will make it to Colorado?" she asked him as she surveyed the carcass of an auto that was Stamp's. "I can see why you call this thing 'The Skunk,'" she added in a gratuitous assessment of the black-and-white 1955 Dodge they were to take on the seven-hundred-mile trip from Glacier to Fort Collins.

"Bite your tongue," he said. "This is a fine piece of driving machinery."

On the night of their departure, there was a party for Marcy and Jim at the Dark River, just outside the town of Saint Mary. Guitars rang out, Stamp played his harmonica, and the sentimental college crowd sang "Blowin' in the Wind."

At midnight, the high point of disequilibrium of the partiers, Stamp leaped to his feet, lifted Marcy to hers, and shouted to their assembled summer friends, "It's been good to know you. But now we have to hit the highway. Big cigars and motor cars."

Away they went, through the trees and away from the river, back to the lodge where The Skunk awaited.

Hance Green followed them to their car, hugged Marcy, and shook Jim's hand. He pressed into the palm of each starry-eyed, tipsy traveler three hundred-dollar bills, which was a huge bonus considering that they made only two hundred dollars per month for working at the lodge.

Mr. Green said, "We've liked having you here at Saint Mary's. You're the only college kids who came out here with the correct attitude and learned to love the native culture of the place. If you don't get too screwed up and go and get married or something foolish like that, we'd be proud to have you back next year or at any time in the future. Now, it's dangerous up on the mountain road at night, so go easy on the speed when you're driving. Good luck."

They drove off into the onyx night, starting the five-thousand-foot ascent through the mountains up to Logan Pass and proceeding over the Going-to-the-Sun Road to the west side of the park. Marcy was elated at the prospect of driving right through the heart of the mountains.

The following day, news reached Saint Mary's of a car plunging over the Going-to-the-Sun Road and into the forest thousands of feet below. The Skunk was recovered by park rangers the next spring after the melt of the forty-foot snowpack in the valley of Granite Mountain. No traces were found of Marcy Manikowski and Jim Stampler, but their bodies had helped the grizzlies make it through the cold and hungry winter, and the park had returned to itself.

Frank Forino

. . .

Childcare

· · ·

Frank Forino was born with a broken arm and two broken collarbones, physical conditions that may have predicted his lifelong history of physical conflict.

His dad, the radio announcer Tom Forino, called the Minneapolis *Tribune*, where they published anything he said, and reported that his wife had given birth to a son—born at 12:12 p.m. on the twelfth day of August (his parents' twelfth wedding anniversary) and weighing in at twelve pounds, twelve ounces. The sole truth in this formulation was that Frank was born on his parents' anniversary. The part that made his mother, Catherine, unhappy was the preposterous claim that she had given birth to a twelve-pound, twelve-ounce baby.

Tom Forino spoiled his son rotten. When little Frank was two, Tom bought him a small record player and several 33 rpm discs. Frank learned a shortcut that became a valuable personal tool in his life: most of life was perception, not reality. By memorizing the colors in the middle border of the records, he was able to convince people that he could read. His parents would invite him to demonstrate this ability of their precocious son to groups of their friends who gathered for parties. The guests sat in a circle around him and witnessed the phenomenon as he sat on the floor reading record labels.

The banker Pennington said, "Will you look at that little fart? He's a genius." He was Jesus in the temple, speaking to a dubiously wise and clearly inebriated group of elders.

After a few weeks of enduring his reading performances, his sister Sheila tried to bust Frank. For his kid records, she substituted her Frank Sinatra and Jo Stafford records with identical label colors. But he had been warned of her treachery by his sister Patricia and, before he was publicly humiliated, he got around the problem by memorizing the patterns of names and title markings on the labels of the substituted discs and matching them with the new songs. So, fairly quickly, before he was again called on to perform for his parents' crowd of friends, he could identify Sinatra's "Summer Wind" and Jo Stafford's "You Belong to Me."

As he grew older, Frank became a graceful, strong boy, with a glorious head of curly hair that his mother insisted be left long. The girls in the neighborhood loved him, especially two of the older girls who lived near the Forino house: Eloise LaFrance, who lived with her rich family directly across the street from the Forinos, and the beautiful Mary Ellen O'Leary from down the street. Both of these girls were three years older than Frank. They teased him constantly, calling him Frankie and telling him they liked his spit curls. He largely ignored their clumsy teasing.

One day, when he was ten years old, he was walking down the street between his house and the red-brick palace of the LaFrance family. He heard giggling from an open rear window of the Buick Roadmaster moored in the street in front of LaFrance's.

"Frankie," came the mirthful voice of Eloise from the back seat of the Buick. "Come on over and get in with us. We're going to tell you the facts of life." Frank didn't know what the phrase "facts of life" meant, but he sensed the concept was something about the opposite sex that he wanted to learn. He quickly moved over to the

Roadmaster and got into the back upholstered seat with the little women for whom he felt a strong affection.

"So," he demanded to know, "what are the facts of life?"

Mary Ellen and Eloise looked at one another, barely able to hold their laughter, each waiting for the other to speak. Finally, Eloise blurted, "The facts of life are that you are a Kotex."

The girls giggled. Frank had never heard of Kotex, but their derision made him break into tears of frustration at being made an object of fun. He jumped out of the car and raced across the street and into his house where his mother was cooking dinner. Catherine Forino asked him what was wrong.

Sobbing, Frank said, "Mary Ellen and Eloise said I'm a Kotex."

Catherine Forino reared back and said sharply, "Don't you ever say that word in this house again, Frank."

One morning, Zavin Triblin, a neighbor child of Yugoslavian refugees, showed up at the Forino house with his mother, and stayed to play with Frank while his mother went to work as a maid in the Griggs house on King's Highway. Zav was small, with dark skin, white teeth, and an alert, somewhat alarmed look. Frank's mom told him that Zav would be staying with them on school days before classes and after the end of the school day until his mom picked him up. She asked Frank to watch after the little guy, and she told Frank that she would give him a quarter for each day completed without injury to either boy. It was his first paying job.

The Triblins joined the local Lutheran church, and one of the men in the congregation who owned a restaurant gave Mr. Triblin a job as a sous chef. This was a big step down from his position as a head chef in a Yugoslavian restaurant, but he accepted it gratefully.

Frank and Zavin started full days of school in fourth grade at Washburn Elementary. Zav continued to wait at the Forino house each day after school until his mother came from her job to pick him up and walk three blocks up to the Triblin home, which was closer to the railroad tracks. In the morning, Mrs. Triblin left Zav off at the Forino house an hour before school so that she could get to her job on time. The boys walked together up the hill—a short way to school. Each day as they emerged from the house, Zavin took Frank's hand and held it tightly as they started out. They were a striking pair—a tall, husky boy with curly hair and glasses leading a small, dark foreigner.

Frank and Zav were assigned to the same class at Washburn. Both tolerated school—Frank with resignation and Zav with growing enthusiasm. Zav's position in school was helped by the facts that he was surpassingly intelligent and clearly the best-behaved student in the class. But socially, things weren't so good for Zav. Like any newcomer, he encountered all types of people, most of them well meaning, but some of whom seemed to be in training to become nasty adults, discovering at school a large field of people on whom to work out the prejudices they had internalized from discussions within their families.

So it was with Jim "Hilex" Roberts, a fifth grader who was a wide pug with an outsized head that looked like the Hilex drops, which looked like enormous plastic heads and were worn by the members of one of the marching units in the Saint Paul Winter Carnival Grand Parade.

Roberts asked Zav, "What's a little jigaboo like you doing at Washburn?"

Zav said, "I'm not a jigaboo. I'm a Slav. What is 'jigaboo'?"

"I don't care what you are: Slav, nigger. You don't belong here at Washburn."

"I belong," said Zav.

Hilex cuffed Zav on the side of the head and knocked him to the ground, but Zav was unhurt and unbowed.

One morning, when throngs of Washburn kids were on the playground for recess, Frank emerged from the back school door, and he thought he heard Zav cry out. Frank used his perch at the top of stairs as a point from which to survey the tangled groups of children dispersed over the playground. In the middle of a scrum, he could see Zav lying on the ground with Hilex looming over him. Frank ripped off his baseball cap and glasses, gave them to his nearest schoolmate, and pushed his way through the crowd to the scene.

As Frank approached the group, Hilex said to him, "What do you want, curly boy Frank? I like your curls."

Without pause, Frank grabbed Zav's assailant around the neck and put him in a headlock and then spun the bubblehead over his hip and onto the asphalt surface of the playground. Frank put his tennis-shoed foot on Hilex's chest with enough pressure to convey the threat that he might stomp on him.

"Tell Zavin you are sorry, Roberts."

When no word was spoken immediately by Hilex, Frank put more weight on his chest. Finally, Hilex Roberts gave up and said, "Sorry, Triblin."

Only then did Frank remove his foot and let Roberts regain his feet. But he gave Roberts one last reminder by punching him in the stomach and again knocking him to the ground. Word got around school that you shouldn't cross Frank Forino or his sidekick, Zavin Triblin. After that point, knowing that he would not likely be harassed gave Zav a sort of freedom to be himself—a new student from a foreign world.

The train tracks ran unguarded behind the Triblin house. In their last two years of elementary school, Frank and Zavin spent many an afternoon lying on the grass bank that sloped down to the tracks. Trains passed in a cloud of steam and a burst of noise, beckoning to take the boys with them down the line. Frank and Zav told each other that someday they would go places by timing it just right and hopping on one of the train cars at a point where there were ladders. But they knew it was just talk; neither of them was reckless enough to try to hitch a ride on a fast-moving train.

One day, in their last year at Washburn, Zavin decided to go places. Frank heard sirens from two blocks away, wailing out a penetrating sound near the Triblin's house. He jumped on his bike and pedaled furiously up the hill. Crowds of people had gathered, and he saw the fearsome sight of the flashing lights of an ambulance and police cars. As he drew near, he saw two medics leaning over Zav, who was on a stretcher, lying still. A third white-gowned man was holding a sheet onto which a nurse deposited gored flesh. In a vision that would always be with him, Frank saw Zavin's bloody leg, separated above the knee, lifted into the sheet like a piece of meat going into a case in a butcher's shop. As he turned away in an involuntary shudder, he felt his mom's hand on his shoulder.

"Don't worry, Frankie. Zavin will be OK. They're taking him to the hospital. Apparently he lost a leg under the wheels of the train, but he's still alive." Zavin did lose his right leg to the speeding train, but the surgery to cap the vital blood vessels and nerves in the stump was successful. He lived. He spent two weeks in the hospital and a month at the Kenny Clinic Rehabilitation Institute learning how to get around on one leg and crutches. After the first week, Frank was allowed to visit Zav in the hospital, accompanied by his mother. When they had both said hello, Frank's mom was good enough to wait outside in the hallway while the two boys talked.

"What happened, Zav?" was the first thing Frank asked. "Did you try to hitch onto the train?"

"Yeah, I almost had it. But I was stupid to try."

"You were pretty brave to do that, if you ask me."

"Brave, no. Dumb, yes," said Zavin, starting to cry. "I should not have tried. But if I was going to try it, I needed you with me to show me how to do it."

"What do you mean? I never would have done it. I don't have the guts."

"You're full of it, Frank. You're the bravest person I have ever known."

By the time that Zavin got out of the hospital, the boys were about to finish elementary school and were looking forward to high school. Frank was signed up at Breck, a college-prep school. Zavin's parents couldn't afford a private school, so he went to Southwest High, part of the very good public school system in Minneapolis. That summer, the boys could be seen walking down the street, Zavin on a pair of crutches at first and, after he got a wooden prosthetic leg from the Kenny Institute, on his feet, trying to learn to walk again with the help of a cane and an arm assist from Frank.

School started the day after Labor Day in the fall. They still spent a lot of time together after classes were finished for the day, but they began to drift apart after the fall of freshman year when Frank started playing junior-varsity hockey. Zavin was usually left to sit at home alone. He didn't try to get into any school activities, and no one encouraged him.

Frank's father heard from his son that Zavin was a lost soul at the huge public high school. He decided to try to get Zav a scholarship to attend the much smaller Breck the following semester. The former radio sports announcer persuaded a few local athletes to kick in tuition money for the poor "crippled kid."

Zav was happy to go to Breck in his sophomore year, and the Breck teachers were pleased to have him. He was a math prodigy. In fact, his prowess as an algebra student moved his advisor to talk him into signing up to participate, beginning in junior year, in a pilot

program run by the University of Minnesota for advanced place-
ment of high-school students with great promise of excellence in
pursuing higher education in scientific and math disciplines. So, in
September of that year, Zav began to attend college-level calculus
and philosophy classes once a week at the university. Making his
way along the crowded sidewalks of the campus in his boiled-wool
cap and a long, quilted coat handed down to him by Frank, leaning
on one leg and limping a bit with each difficult step, he looked like
a hobbled little monk.

Zav became a favorite among his university teachers for his as-
tounding academic ability. His calculus instructor, a recent master's
degree graduate in math, spoke to his department chairman about
Zav, saying the kid was as philosophically insightful as anyone he
had ever encountered, including fellow grad students and senior
professors.

Zavin knew he was a good math student, but he couldn't quite
understand all the fuss over his ability. Since his family had moved to
the United States, and particularly since he became disabled, he had
been put down so often for his slow gait, his foreign looks, and his
ineptitude in American colloquial speech and manners that nothing
that he could do seemed of much value. But the university math and
philosophy departments made a fuss over Zav. They contacted the
teachers at Breck and reminded them to keep an eye on this boy: he
was going to be something.

Zav was chosen for the Breck quiz-bowl team, which competed
against all Minnesota high schools on the basis of the ability to answer unscripted questions, calling for answers ranging from geogra-
phy to politics. After playoff contests, the Breck team made it to the
state quiz-bowl tournament held in the rotunda of the Minnesota
state capitol building in Saint Paul.

On the day of the state quiz-bowl meet, Zavin was surprised to see not only Frank Forino but the entire Forino family in the audience in one of the front rows. Four teams made it to the semifinals, including Breck, two other Minneapolis schools, and Central, an outstanding public school from Saint Paul. Breck won its first match against Roosevelt High School and ended up in the finals against Saint Paul Central. After a very close contest, it came down to what was called the essay portion of the event. The question was how the practice of politics arose. The Breck students huddled briefly and asked Zav to try to give an answer. Zavin answered confidently. He said that, as the philosopher Aristotle had written, humans were social beings whose fundamental need was for contact with other humans, so it followed that they were also intrinsically political beings with a strong innate desire to participate with their fellow citizens in their own government. This answer won the day for Breck and moved the head of the panel of judges to remark that Zavin Triblin's answer was remarkably perceptive and rested on a feel for philosophy that was rare in a person his age.

On commencement day from Breck, as the student with the highest grade point average in the graduating class, Zavin delivered the valedictory speech to the students and their guests. As he made his limping way up to the stage, a few wise-guy students seated behind the Forinos jeered in an audible way at Zav's gait and his diminutive stature.

"There goes the cricket," said one of the loudmouths. Frank Forino turned and stared at them intensely until one of them nodded and apologized. Someone lowered the microphone for Zavin, and he mounted the platform behind the speakers' podium. He began by recognizing the teachers in a most gracious way. He said that they had turned his life from a lonely existence to one alive with books and the love of learning. To his classmates, Zav spoke like an older brother, delivering in his understated style the message that each of them was a fortunate person who could pursue his or her dreams. He ended to thunderous and surprised applause by saying a most unusual thing to be uttered by a high-school student in the year 1970: everyone should pray for the soldiers who fought and died on both sides in the "tragically mistaken" war in Vietnam.

Young Gun

. . .

LIKE MANY COLLEGE KIDS, FRANK Forino had no idea what he wanted to do with his life. Fresh from his sophomore-year hockey season, in which the University of Minnesota came in second in the conference, his coach, Red Feeley, called him into his office and whistled when he draped his large frame into a chair.

"Fonty," the coach said, "you're a big, strong kid: as the tale of the tape has it, six feet three inches and two hundred and ten pounds. For Christ's sake, you could be a really great college player, rather than just a good one, and maybe even a pro prospect. But as you well know, you don't practice and train hard enough. And I know you're not great academically. You don't seem like a guy who's ready to settle down. I'm going to tell you what: If I were your age, and as good looking and talented as you are, I'd get my butt out to Hollywood and try to secure some acting tryouts. You'll get some casting calls after you hang around and meet people. If you don't get any chances, I have a friend out there who will help out."

Frank went to Los Angeles. He didn't find a job in acting right away, but he got a job as an attendant at a fitness gym, where he met a rich older guy named Jimmy Arrigone, who said he needed another bodyguard. After getting to know Frank, Arrigone offered him a full-time job to provide him with security, and Frank jumped at the opportunity.

One of Frank's first projects for Mr. Arrigone involved the Roberto brothers, two real-estate investors who had recently moved to LA.

The Roberto brothers arrived at the Los Angeles private airport Millionaires Terminal at six in the morning; they were in a hurry to get to Denver to close on a contract to rebuild a bridge over the intersection of two interstate highways. As their pilots pulled their Citation jet out of the hanger, Tom Roberto stood at the terminal window admiring its glinting navy-blue finish with the lightning bolt and the silver name Tanson Company on the fuselage. He noticed that the private plane from the adjoining hangar was pulled out and parked over the line marking their space.

"Herman," he said, "go out there and see if you can find the caretaker of the *Zeus* or *Seuss* or whatever the hell the name is of the plane parked on our space. Tell him we own the Tanson hangar and tell him to get his goddamn plane out of our space."

Herman gave his brother a baleful look. "Tom, they're barely over the line onto our space, and we'll be gone for the day. Let's just overlook it."

"All right, I'll do it myself," Tom said, with the resigned, huffy air of one who had come to expect others, including his brother, to perform small or unpleasant tasks for him. He strode out the terminal door. Herman watched him out the window. Tom went into the hangar and appeared outside moments later with a bucket in one hand and a paintbrush in the other. Were it not for the gray silk suit he wore, which Herman knew to be a thirty-five-hundred-dollar Armani from Rodeo Drive, Tom could have been confused for the plump little Dutch Boy painter.

The next thing Herman saw was his brother painting bright yellow over the white lines marking the Robertos' berth. Tom bent down and hopped backward with his legs spread wide, running the paintbrush along behind him. At the first square corner of the lines, Tom made a quick turn, inadvertently drawing the paintbrush over the top of one of his alligator shoes and marking it with a wide yellow stripe. Herman could almost read Tom's lips calling down eternal damnation on the trespasser. He burst into tears of laughter.

Tom stormed back into the terminal, sat on a leather couch, and pulled a copy of the *Wall Street Journal* off a table. He threw open the paper in front of his face and said nothing. Herman assumed a solemn look and tried not to laugh. Finally Tom lowered the paper, glowered at Herman, and said, "Don't say a fucking word."

A voice came over a terminal loudspeaker notifying the Robertos that their plane was ready, and the pilots were prepared to take off. Simultaneously, a young man in uniform appeared. He took their two briefcases and led them out to the plane.

Jake, their second officer, was at the foot of the fold-down stairs and took their bags. He had a concerned look on his face as he greeted the brothers.

"Good morning," he said in an overly loud voice. Then, as an almost-whispered aside to Tom, he said, "I'm sorry, Mr. Roberto; there was nothing we could do."

Tom was perplexed as he walked up the stairs. He assumed Jake was referring to the delay in departure, but when he got to the top of the stairs, he was confronted with the obvious cause of the pilot's concern. A big, broad-shouldered man dressed in a blue suit and yellow tie faced them with a smile and a drawn handgun. "Please step into your plane, Roberto brothers," he said. "And, in doing so, watch your step very carefully. We don't want this hammer to strike, do we?"

Tom immediately asserted himself with unwise disdain in his voice. "Who the hell are you, meatball?" he said. "Do you know who we are?"

In answer, the gunman gave Tom a sharp jab to the gut, which sat him down quickly, his hands clutching his stomach. He threw up in a spurt, soiling his pant legs and his shoes.

"Now, look what you did; you barfed on your freshly painted shoes. Yeah, I was watching you do the lines, you silly son of a bitch," the man said, laughing.

In the meantime, Tom was coughing and trying to catch his breath. He couldn't comprehend what was going on. The others—Herman, Jake, and their chief pilot—gazed at the scene with blank faces.

"All right," said the gunman, "I'm Frank Forino, and I'm the new boss of this flight. As pilots, Jake and Chris here know better than to screw with me, another pilot. Just so you know, your plans have changed. Instead of going to Denver, we're all going to Las Vegas so you Robertos can see my boss, Jimmy Arrigone, who just moved into a new building in Lake Las Vegas. He's a great guy, my boss, and I know you'll like him. If you don't act too much like assholes, you'll get a chance to talk with him, and he won't hurt you."

The pilots had already revised their flight plan, faxed it to the FAA, and advised the control tower, which had given them new take-off instructions. They eased the sleek plane out to their assigned runway waiting area. Forino was in the third seat in the passenger cabin, having confiscated a gun from Tom, a serious-looking pistol. He told them to stay buckled in their seats and not to make a move while he went up to the cockpit to talk to the pilots or, he said, he'd stuff their shorts down their throats.

When the plane reached an altitude of fifteen thousand feet, Forino returned to the cabin. He rearranged the seating so that the brothers were facing aft and he was facing forward, looking into their faces and beyond them to the cockpit, the door to which he told the pilots to leave open so that he could see and hear them.

"Now, boys, take off your coats and relax. What do you have on hand to drink?" Forino asked. He rose and was directed by Herman Roberto straight to the liquor locker. "I'm having a tequila straight. How about you guys?"

Tom was so indignant and angry that he could barely speak. "We don't drink tequila or anything else in the morning," he said, looking at his watch.

"I'll have a shot of Cuervo Gold," said Herman in a soft voice.

Tom glared at him as if he had switched sides.

Frank Forino laughed. "Jose Cuervo shooter coming up for the brother who didn't boot."

When Forino sat down, he handed the tequila shot glass to Herman. He raised his own glass in a toast, smiling broadly.

Tom wore a sour smell and expression. He spoke to Forino in a less but still-belligerent tone. "Are you sure you know who we are?" he said, rather too loudly under the circumstances.

"I know all about you," said Frank. "You're two little pimps who stole your daddy's business up north, fired your sister, dumped your wives, and came out to LA to make some real money and, I'll bet, to see if you could get lucky with some of the Southern California silicone sweethearts. Well, how have you done, gentlemen? From what I've heard, your business is good, probably better than you expected. But your efforts with babes haven't worked out so well, which would be my bet for a couple of mutts like you."

"None of this is any of your business, Mr. Forina," said Tom, deliberately mispronouncing Forino.

Frank pulled off his suit coat, revealing a leather shoulder holster with the gun snugly holstered. "Mr. Roberto, you are a real annoying piece of work. Do you ever act normal?"

"It's tough with an ape like you sitting in my plane ordering me around. Besides, normal would mean you'd be dead right now," said Tom.

"My boss asked me not to spank you too hard before we get to Las Vegas. I'm going to try to follow his wishes, but you are making it hard for me. I warn you: you don't want to piss me off anymore. Understand?" said Frank, directing a hard look at Tom.

"I get it," Tom said sullenly, and then he fell into a silence that lasted the rest of the flight. Herman and Forino talked amiably and played gin on a table between their chairs.

After they touched down in Las Vegas, Frank Forino went up to the cockpit to make sure the pilots knew where the millionaires' private plane terminal was and where they should pull in.

The plane taxied into a demarcated spot in front of a huge hangar marked with a sign that said "Tucci-Arrigone." As they came to a stop and the engines were shut down, Frank Forino went up to the cockpit and announced over the speaker, "All right, all of you. We're here to visit Mr. Jimmy Arrigone, the owner of the new Pearl Hotel on Lake Las Vegas. We'll ride out there in Mr. Arrigone's car, which will be here to pick us up in a few minutes. Try to be cool, and maybe you won't be hurt too bad."

The trip from the airport to Lake Las Vegas was made in silence. Frank sat in the front seat with the driver. The Robertos and the two pilots sat in the four back seats of the Hummer limo. On the way, Herman had another tequila shot, to the displeasure of his brother, who shook his head and muttered, "Dumb shit."

Their arrival at the Pearl was greeted with hostile stares, as if they were gambling-industry regulators there for an inspection. Frank took them to the penthouse elevator, where he turned a security key in a lock and motioned to the Robertos to enter. On the way up to the penthouse, he spoke as though he were a Vatican functionary preparing a group with last-minute tips of proper decorum for a Papal audience, explaining to the brothers specifics of rules they must observe when they entered the presence of Jimmy Arrigone.

"Now, listen to me. You two schmucks will be talking to Mr. Arrigone for whatever time on whatever subjects he wants. Keep your mouths shut unless he asks you to talk. You understand?" Frank glared at them like a harshly restrained beast. Tom and Herman had dealt with sidemen like Frank. They were dangerous people, because violence was their instinct and their habit. Tom nonetheless spoke to Frank with a certain superiority that he assumed with any underling.

"Look, Mr. Forino, what the hell does Jimmy Arrigone want us for? He's a big Vegas cheese, and we're two construction guys making an honest living building bridges and roads," Tom said.

"Does the name of Father Henri Blecker ring a bell?"

"No. Should it?"

"How about the name of an attorney? Your sister's lawyer— Martin Waite? Remember him?" Frank asked with a grin. "You two are high on my boss's shit list for circulating some bullshit about Father Blecker being a pedophile, thus threatening to hurt the reputation of the Father, who is a very close friend of Mr. Waite and a friend and restaurant customer of Mr. Arrigone's business associate, Rico Tucci of Boston."

They had arrived at the seventeenth-floor penthouse of the Pearl Hotel. Just before the elevator doors opened, Frank added, "Just watch your mouths."

They stepped off the elevator into a vast room covered with a black-and-white chessboard marble floor. The room contained several working fountains, high ceilings, cut-glass chandeliers, and statues depicting gargoyles and nude bodies in various strained poses. The desk of Jimmy Arrigone sat on a pedestal at the far end of the room, facing away from the drapeless windows so that the morning sun backlit the wispy sprigs of hair sticking out from his head like rays emanating from the head of the Sun King.

Arrigone did not rise or otherwise acknowledge the presence of the Robertos. His gaze was fixed on a small coin on his desk, which he was viewing through a magnifying lens.

Tom Roberto finally spoke to attract his attention. "What is going on? Your man Frank here broke into our plane and hijacked us. What the fuck do you want?"

The profanity uttered by Tom caused the great man to look up in surprise.

"All right, let's talk about your behavior," said Jimmy. "You have tried to ruin the name of Father Blecker for some nonsense about diddling with children. The Father is a close friend of my associate, Rico Tucci. Rico asked me to stop you, so I'm asking myself, 'What can I do to make you stop?' I could stop you from working on any more construction projects. I could rough you up or maybe just make you disappear. Or—and this is what I think I've decided to do, depending on your attitude—I could ask you to stop because you are hurting an innocent man of God and a friend of my close friend Rico. Will that work?"

Tom looked up at Arrigone and, as always, spoke for Herman and himself. "We don't know a Father Becker or Blecker or whatever the name is."

Jimmy came down three steps from his desk pedestal. At a height of about five feet two inches, he looked like the Penguin from the Batman movies.

"Listen to me, Mr. Roberto. You do know or know of Father Blecker. Understand?" he said, drawing so close that Tom had to step back to see the little man. "Blecker is a witness in a case involving the lawyer Waite, who became a friend of Rico Tucci through his association with Father Blecker. Rico says you want to cause trouble for Blecker and that you've chosen to do it by sponsoring some story about the priest's supposed thing for little boys."

"That is wrong," said Tom. "Waite is nothing to us but our sister's lawyer."

"He's trying to make you pay your sister for cutting her out of your new company. Am I right?"

Tom now approached Jimmy to establish a man-to-man connection. That moved Frank Forino, who was standing behind Tom, to grab the back of his suit coat and pull the fabric so hard that Tom was left wearing what looked like a rubber wet suit. Tom stood in resignation.

"I don't know how you would be aware of that phony lawsuit," said Tom, "but now I'll have reason to sue my sister and her lawyer, Waite, for slander. And I'm happy to leave your priest friend alone, because I don't know who he is anyway."

Jimmy Arrigone stepped back and kicked up his foot like a miniature drum major, catching Tom in the groin and dropping him to the marble floor, where he spit up his food for the second time that day.

Tom lay on the floor clutching himself. Jimmy stood over him, smiling.

He said, "Now, get these sleds out of here, Frank. But remember this, gentlemen: You do know Father Blecker, and you are going to get off Blecker's ass the press hounds and the family that I understand has been encouraged to complain about him. If you do not, my friend Rico will feel bad, and then I will feel bad, and then you will feel real bad—if you ever feel anything again."

With that, Jimmy toed up to his throne, and Frank dragged Tom to his feet and ushered the Robertos to the elevator.

Forino and The Waites

· · ·

AFTER THEIR STAY AT THE home of Nancy's parents in San Francisco, Martin and Nancy Waite went to Cabo San Lucas for a midcourse honeymoon. They donned their swimwear even before unpacking.

Adopting a Cabo-vacation rhythm, they hit the beach daily at noon. Beginning at one o'clock, the snack shacks on the sand sold bottles of Corona beer packed in tin tubs of crushed ice and served with fresh Mexican lime wedges stuck down the gullets of the bottles. As soon as Martin and Nancy sat in their wooden-framed chairs, which were hung with yellow, red, and orange hues of woven fabric, they were promptly fallen upon by squadrons of Mexican children selling religious statues and other trinkets. They beat the little beggars off with threats—and finally with cash—and then sipped the tooth-cracking beer for relief from the ninety-degree midafternoon heat. The result was, inevitably, a nap.

On their second day on the beach, they dozed until a man's sandal stepped on Waite's bare toes with enough pressure to get his attention. He looked up, shielding his eyes with a hand salute, to see a large Americano looking down at him, smiling amiably. Judging by his size, he could have been a heavyweight boxer or an enforcer out of *The Godfather*. The big guy introduced himself as Frank Forino, an associate of Rico Tucci and Jimmy Arrigone, who sat in a tented cabana fifty feet above them on the beach. Waite peered behind him and saw the bald head of a man peeking out through a cabana door. The man waved a wristy come-on with his fingers, as a bell captain would to a bellboy.

Waite roused Nancy from her sun-glazed sleep, and they followed Frank Forino up to the place of Tucci, who rose to greet them. As he got to his feet, Nancy noted that Tucci was a handsome older man, with black and gray hair and muscled arms. In the chair next to Tucci's was the diminutive pear-shaped person of Jimmy Arrigone. Mr. Arrigone did not rise, and it looked to Waite as if he would not have been capable of summoning the balance and strength to rise out of his awning chair. But Arrigone welcomed them warmly with handshakes and a hand kiss for Nancy, who gazed down upon the curious little man with an aggrieved look as if his kiss may have infected her with warts.

"So, you are the Waites? I am Enrico Tucci, and this is my partner, Jimmy Arrigone. We're happy to meet you," Tucci said for both men.

"Mr. Waite, how is our old friend, the Monsignor Blecker?" asked Arrigone.

"Pardon me," said Tucci. "Can our man Frank get you anything?"

"I would like a beer if you have it," said Waite. "Nancy, what would you like?"

"One more beer, and I'll have to be carried out," said Nancy. "How about a glass of soda water with a lime?"

"Can do," said Frank Forino, appraising Nancy as if she were a ripe pear.

"To answer your question, Mr. Arrigone, Father Blecker is fine. Do you know him?"

"Frank took an airplane ride with the defendants in one of your cases, the Robertos," Arrigone said. "He brought them to see me in Las Vegas, and I had a talk with them about Monsignor Blecker. It was hard for them to take it in at first, I would say, but I think they understood after our discussion that they should never again encourage the crazy family that was claiming that Blecker was a kid pervert. We were told later that Father Blecker was not going to be bothered again. Have you heard anything different?"

"I have a hunch that the lawyer for one of our litigation code-fendants, Royal Reed Securities, may still cause trouble for Father Blecker."

"What's the name of this big-shot lawyer?" Jimmy Arrigone asked.

Waite had to give it some thought before telling Jimmy the name. He didn't want any violence to befall the attorney, Lawrence Lareau.

"You know," said Waite, "I really don't think there will be any more trouble. It might be better to just let it go."

Jimmy gave Waite a sharp look, which Waite took to mean that it was probably not wise to lecture Jimmy Arrigone about what he should or should not do. And a little scare might serve to get the other side moving toward settlement. So Waite gave him the name of Lareau.

Rico Tucci spoke. "We'll leave this Lareau alone for now. But tell us if he as much as hints at bringing up the pedophile stuff again. And, as I think about it, let's have Frank and his guys pay a visit to those Robertos and give them a little refresher course."

"Maybe the Los Angeles Gelato Twins, Frankie," Jimmy said, laughing quietly.

Frank Forino had briefly stepped out of the room and donned a silk Mexican shirt; he now departed as silently as a cat.

It was unclear who the boss was between Jimmy and Rico; they seemed to share their power. Deference was paid to Jimmy. But a brief word from Rico and the dogs had been set on the Robertos. Waite only hoped the dogs—the Gelato Twins—were not so savage as to somehow invite inquiry about any connection between Father Blecker and the duo of Tucci and Arrigone.

Waite said, "It would not be good if there is a lot of trouble and Father Blecker's name gets involved. We may be close to a settlement, and we are in a delicate position."

Rico Tucci said, "Don't worry. We know about delicacy in these matters. By the way, you give me the word and we will do whatever further you want to encourage settlement."

Waite and Nancy were both uneasy with the implication that they would use force as a means of encouragement. Almost in unison, they said that they had to get going.

"Sit," said Jimmy Arrigone, with more demand than invitation in his voice. "Have some champagne with us, please."

Tucci filled the glasses, and champagne was in their hands instantly. "Now, tell us about yourselves," Jimmy Arrigone said, as if he was the head of a college-admissions committee speaking to applicants.

"Well now," interjected Tucci, "we know a bit about Marty. He's a trial lawyer on the rise. He is a close friend of Monsignor Blecker. I would like to hear about the young lady, Nancy."

They waited for Nancy to speak. It was an uneasy feeling, having these two old gangsters staring at her, waiting for her comment.

"I'm another boring wife of just another lawyer, gentlemen. There's nothing interesting about me."

"You should not say your husband is 'just a lawyer,'" Tucci said. "I would like my son to go into law, but he doesn't have enough ambition to do the schoolwork it takes to become a lawyer."

Waite and Nancy finally escaped the hospitality of Jimmy and Rico and retreated back to their room. They fell on the bed and slipped into a sleep induced by beer and champagne.

When they awoke, it was nine o'clock and dark outside. They experienced the surreal sensation of wondering if they had slept around the clock. Nancy was hungover, and both of them were dazed and hungry. Fortunately, the outdoor restaurant of the Melia Hotel served until ten o'clock, so they freshened up, threw clothes on, and hustled outside to the courtyard for dinner.

Like seawater to castaways, they were brought margaritas. They sat at a table looking out at the ocean, their fellow diners only shadowy torchlit presences.

Nancy thought she saw Tucci and Arrigone at a corner table along the ocean balcony. She whispered, "Those creeps are following us around."

Waite glanced over to see Rico waving a bejeweled finger at him. He nodded, smiling.

Waite said, "They are following you around; I just happen to be your date."

"That is just great," Nancy said. "Seriously, how do you know those characters? They seem more than a little suspicious."

"I don't really know them. They are apparently friends of my old college economics teacher, Father Blecker, and they don't like the fact that the Roberto brothers are trying to set him up for pedophilia—which makes Tucci and Arrigone our common allies. It's complicated. I'll tell you all about it some time."

"Tell me now, will you? I have this feeling that you and, I suppose, I are somehow getting into their evil bed."

"I think you're getting the wrong idea. These guys are friends of Father Blecker, so they must be fine."

Thinking to buy a drink for them, Waite peered over to the table where he had seen the old boys, but by then they were being led out the side veranda door by two bulky assistants.

A few days later on the beach, Frank Forino showed up again and escorted them back to the cabana. They were welcomed warmly by the old boys, both of whom gave them looks that spoke deeply of connivance.

"So have you heard about the Robertos?" Rico Tucci asked.

"No, we have not," said Waite. "What about them?"

"It seems they were not on the up and up. They're going to lose the contract and the cost bond they had posted on the Coronado Bay Bridge," said Rico, smiling widely.

"Contract breach?" asked Waite.

"Nothing so simple," said Frank Forino. "The concrete in the bridge road turns out to be mostly sand. One of their subs on the concrete supply side of things, who is one of my colleagues on other deals, bitched to the federal highway people about the heavy sand proportion in the concrete mix, and the Robertos had him roughed up in retaliation. Can you imagine that? So we had to protect our friend, and fortunately Forino's friends, the Gelato Brothers, happened to be in LA. The Robertos both ended up in the hospital with a few broken bones—facial bones. Too bad."

"And the worst problem they have is that the federal district attorney in Los Angeles will be investigating them for fraudulent government contracting," said Rico.

Frank Forino beamed. "Isn't it beautiful?" he said. "They'll never again say anything about Father Blecker."

Jimmy added, "Anyway, their word about anything will be ignored in the future."

Waite accepted a glass of wine and joined in toasting to the bad fortune of the Robertos. Nancy joined in, skeptical though she was about their new friends.

Near the end of their Cabo stay, Waite and Nancy spent increasingly longer periods in their beach chairs, rising to walk the sand only when their skin began to char.

Waite thought that, to be polite, he and Nancy should arrange to do something social with Tucci and Arrigone. When he called to propose that they get together, Rico insisted they all meet for drinks and dinner that evening at his condominium on the beach.

They were shown into an ornate two-floor condo with an atrium encircled by a brass-fenced balcony on the second level. From the top of the two-story ceiling hung a dazzling crystal chandelier that Frank said was taken from the Manhattan townhouse of a debtor of Tucci.

Frank Forino took an inordinate amount of time helping Nancy remove the cotton sweater she had worn against the modest chill of the tropical evening breeze.

"I've seen you in some ads, ma'am," said Forino eagerly. "Perhaps jewelry or perfumes?"

"I think not."

Jimmy Arrigone stepped up and interrupted Nancy's chat with Forino.

"Frank, could you see to the other guests?" he said. "Nancy, I hope Frank didn't ask if you were a Victoria's Secret model. He seems to think all beautiful women should be underwear models."

It struck Nancy that Jimmy Arrigone had the leeching look of a small-time photographer not unhappy to encounter inexperienced young women. She tried to move away from him, but he followed her. Jimmy took her by the arm and led her over to Rico Tucci, who sat in a high, thoroughly un-Mexican wingback chair brought to Cabo from Boston. Nancy's hand was quickly enfolded in Tucci's large mitt and sloppily kissed.

A large man in a black suit, probably one of Tucci and Arrigone's guys and surely not a caterer by trade, approached them with a tray of full champagne glasses. Rico guided Nancy to a chair next to his wingback.

"So I assume your husband is going to settle his class action with Royal Reed?" Rico said.

Nancy paused briefly and then said, "He doesn't comment on pending litigation."

He laughed. "Look, young lady, my only interest in the case, besides meeting Marty and now your lovely self, is to make sure no one hurts one of the witnesses: Monsignor Blecker."

"I don't think anyone will mess with Father Blecker if you're involved. I sure wouldn't—I can tell you that," said Nancy.

"Oh? And why is that? Would you be afraid of two old guys like Jimmy and me?"

Nancy quickly said, "I would be, and I am." She knew instinctively that nothing could make them more content than the knowledge that they were feared.

The evening went quickly, with drinks followed by an elaborate buffet featuring langouste lobsters and marlin steaks. Waite amused the group with the story of finding himself in bed with Nancy's parents on their recent trip to San Francisco.

In all, it was a pleasant-enough evening that passed without incident, which had been Martin's hope. The interesting thing was that, for all the adventures they must have experienced, the old boys had few stories to tell, perhaps because they knew many secrets whose purposeful or unintended revelation could bring disaster on them and on succeeding generations of their own flesh.

Frank thought they could be excused for being secretive and for being weary of bearing the weight of the constant peril that was part of the lives they led.

Making the Market Work

• • •

Jimmy Arrigone leaned on Frank Forino to get into a legitimate business as a personal hedge against the risks of the Tucci-Arrigone "family enterprises," which were under constant scrutiny and often investigation by federal and state prosecutors.

Forino resisted leaving Las Vegas, where he had a lot of time to play golf and relax when he wasn't performing the hard-guy roles that Arrigone assigned to him. But there was no resisting the wishes of Arrigone or his partner, Rico Tucci. So, despite the fact that he had never finished his undergraduate training, Frank found himself enrolled in and was quickly granted a bachelor's degree in an online program, a development that Mr. Tucci facilitated on an expedited basis.

Soon after that, Rico Tucci somehow got Frank a job as an associate investment banker at Royal Reed Securities in Manhattan. All the other new associates at the firm had MBAs from prominent schools, so it was a wonder that Frank got the job without having even been granted an undergraduate degree from a real college. At the request of Mr. Tucci, he was assigned a small private office with a window, unlike the other first-year associates with whom he started who worked in a bull pen of small portable enclosures. All it took was Tucci's word for Forino to be treated as if he were a partner at Royal Reed.

Forino stared out at the East River from his office on the sixtieth floor of Ten Wall Street. The sky was clear enough, and Forino's head was sufficiently foggy to permit him to see all the way back in time and place to his girlfriend's family's summer house on Lake Minnetonka, west of Minneapolis. Beach parties drifted back to him hazily, like breaking wisps of smoke. Judy Torentelli's bikini was red and small. The band did its best to cover Beatles songs.

His daydreams were broken off by the institutional buzz of his phone. In response to his phone call to try to arrange a time to talk to Bill Graebner, the head of corporate finance, Bill's secretary said she wanted to schedule a meeting with him. He felt lucky to get an appointment for a meeting, because Graebner had shown little interest in him. The secretary said they would have lunch in Graebner's office at twelve thirty the next Monday.

This gave Forino the weekend to worry about how to make his request to Graebner for a work assignment. He wanted to ask that he be assigned to assist in responding to a request by the Vatican for a proposal by Royal Reed and several large investment banks to do some unspecified investment-banking work for the Catholic Church in the United States. Forino squirmed through the weekend. Not until Sunday night did he try to write out an outline of his thoughts for the Graebner meeting set for the next day. He didn't know what the agenda of the meeting would be, but he hoped it would not involve a discussion of his connection with Tucci and Arrigone and of any attempt to leverage his connection with them to try to get business for Royal Reed.

When he showed up at Bill Graebner's office for lunch, Bill lunged out of his chair like a pulling football guard. He seized Forino's right hand with both of his own mitts and pumped it in an elliptical motion.

Bill was a wide, neatly dressed man with a cement smile. "Mr. Forino," he said, "nice to see you. You have a really firm handshake. I like that in a man. Football?"

"I played a bit of hockey in college, Mr. Graebner."

Graebner said, "You've made a favorable impression here at Royal Reed. And I can see why: a clean-cut young man such as you with a great background. How do you like it here?"

"I enjoy it very much," Frank said.

As they spoke, Graebner assumed his natural place behind his big desk, and Forino sat in one of the side chairs. He scanned Graebner's office walls for power photos, expecting the kind taken with politicians and other notables that typically hung on the walls of business executives' offices. But the photos on the wall looked like shots of Bill and his family in posed groups. It looked to Forino as though the pictures covered a long span of time, showing Bill's family members at various ages. It was either that or Bill had a huge family. There were many pictures. As it turned out, Graebner had three groups of children borne by his three wives, Jane the First, Sally, and Jane the Younger—as Bill called his present wife in emblem of the man's virility and of his ability to neatly arrange things.

"Let's discuss the Vatican's request for a proposal from us to do investment-banking work," Graebner said. "I got a call from my old friend, Enrico Tucci, the Boston restaurateur, who somehow knows that the Vatican is going to interview us to do some banking tasks for them. He wants me to include you on the team assigned to work on our effort to get this business."

Frank said, "You're way ahead of me. I requested this meeting to ask you if you thought I have enough experience to be part of that team. But I want you to know that I don't want to be on the pitch team because of my connection with Mr. Tucci and Mr. Arrigone."

Graebner stared at him for a period long enough to make Frank wonder if he said something wrong or if the man had suffered a stroke.

"Thank you for coming in. I'll get back to you" Bill said as he pushed back from his big desk and reached across to shake Forino's hand with his own enormous hand.

Frank left Bill Graebner's office without lunch and, he suspected, without a job at Royal Reed for disclaiming his intent to employ the influence of Tucci and Arrigone. But when he returned to his office, he had a message to go back to Graebner's office at three o'clock that afternoon to continue their discussion.

When he went back to Bill's office, he was shown to a side conference room. Graebner met him at the door and, taking him by the elbow, introduced him to John Thornton, a sallow-looking guy who was one of the investment bank's in-house lawyers.

"Now," Graebner said, "I've been thinking about the fact that, as a new Royal Reed employee, you have become one of us. And in addition to your fine educational background, you have what we consider to be a special qualification: first, you bring with you the imprimatur and, I hope, the persuasive power of Tucci-Arrigone. So I've asked one of our lawyers, Thornton here, to give you a little primer on how we can use the power of your connections without sacrificing anyone's integrity. I'm going to excuse myself for a while, and you and Thornton can talk. I'll be back."

After Graebner's departure Thornton said, "So, Mr. Forino, we're told that your patrons—Tucci and Margionne—can make anyone, including the Catholic Church, do what they want."

Forino sat up straight in his chair and fixed his gaze directly on the lawyer. "Let's get something straight up front: the names are Enrico Tucci and Jimmy Arrigone, not 'Margionne.' I would suggest you memorize those names. Secondly, they are not my patrons; they are my former employers and my friends. And finally, while they have influence and are persuasive, they do not make anyone do anything. You understand that?"

"I do. I meant no disrespect. Now let me help you understand something about how a major investment bank such as Royal Reed conducts its business. If and when you work on the effort to secure the Vatican as an investment-banking business, you will be working with the chief executive of this bank, Paul McHugh. No matter how much you may wish to join in any discussions or other actions, you will follow Mr. McHugh's lead in all things. And recognize that we would not in any way be connected with anything that could be construed as a use of extra-business power. Do you see what I mean?"

"I'll be discreet, as I always am," said Frank.

Paul McHugh and his wife, Natalie, went to Switzerland to attend an investment-banking conference of the Big Eight world economic powers. The conference was in Geneva, the international banking capital of Europe. Switzerland was the home of huge banks and continued to maintain their famous numbered depository accounts where, it is thought, billions of units of various currencies are on the books of banks or rest in lockboxes, some part of it waiting for owners whose wars and lives were long since lost.

Mike Rosenbloom, Royal Reed's general counsel; Bill Graebner, head of corporate finance; and Frank Forino accompanied Paul on the trip in one of the Royal Reed Gulfstream jets. After the conference, the other Royal Reed representatives and Mrs. McHugh had taken a commercial flight from Geneva back to New York. Paul McHugh and Forino kept the company plane and moved on to Rome, where they met a Royal Reed local banker to prepare for the next morning's meeting with the managing director of the Vatican Bank.

The Vatican business offices were not in the style of the flamboyantly ornate ancient and historic public and religious spaces. They were down two floors underground in large, well-lit rooms with a modern, subtle business ambience.

They were taken to Anselmo Conti. Mr. McHugh, Frank, and a local Royal Reed man who could speak both Italian and English, there to act as the interpreter, entered an ornate office. Signor Conti sat behind a giant, carved wooden desk and greeted them in perfect

English. It turned out that Conti was educated at Princeton as an undergrad and at Stanford Business School. He had been brought in to manage the bank at the time of a scandal in which the Vatican's financial affairs were examined by public authorities and found to be wanting. After that time, when it was widely believed that the bank was insolvent and would be forced into bankruptcy, things changed dramatically. A twenty-billion-dollar private equity financing was arranged by a consortium of international banks. It was rumored that the loan facility had been fully collateralized by real estate around the world owned by Roman Catholic episcopates and by the Holy See itself, a fact that offered an interesting peek into the vast wealth of the Catholic Church.

"Mr. Conti," Paul McHugh asked, "may we know the nature of your disagreement with your present investment banker?"

Conti began deliberately clenching his hands and obviously measuring the matter for a moment. "As I'm sure you know, Lazard Freres has been our lead banker out of its New York office. I hesitate to, and will not, say there was anything wrong with Lazard or our banking arrangement. Let me summarize it this way. Our lead Lazard banker has gone part time in the past few years and has been handling us as one of his few remaining major accounts. He is now retiring fully. After that time, Lazard had in mind a plan to operate our account out of Milan under the management of a younger man whom we do not know well enough. That would be inconvenient for us. We are therefore seeking a new investment banker."

"So, you are not moving because of some disagreement with Lazard?"

"I would say that is a fair statement, except for one point that we thought we had settled but apparently had settled only with the departing partner on our account and not with the Lazard Bank. When the Vatican does business, it does so as a sovereign state with unique but fundamentally private and temporal characteristics and with, by far, the most wealth of any church on earth. At the same time, it is the seat of government of the world's largest religion with the greatest number of adherents to one faith.

"The Vatican has normal diplomatic relations with more countries than any other state. It is neutral in war and in international disputes. It is the one sovereign state concerned with moral principle in the interest of all people of the world. This unique position of the Vatican must be protected from attack, from financial crisis, from moral decay, and from associations or alliances, real or apparent, that could endanger its reputation in any way. For that reason, one understanding we must have with our chief financial advisor is that we have the right to veto its taking as a client any government or major organization that, by association, has the potential to sully our world position or limit or harm us."

Paul had trouble assimilating the notion that any large investment bank could enter into this kind of arrangement.

"Tell me," he said. "Has the Vatican had such agreements in the past with investment banks? If so, may I read a copy of the contractual language you have used in this regard?"

"The past agreements are confidential, but if we decide to proceed with you, our lawyers will provide draft language for your review," said Conti.

Paul asked for a personal break to go to the bathroom and to talk to Frank. But it was also to try to recover from the shock that a prospective client, albeit a large one, was asking for a veto over the future business Royal Reed could take, and had the gall in the next breath to say that it would supply contractual language to this effect if it decided that it wanted to engage Royal Reed.

In the hallway outside the restroom, Paul said to Frank, "What do you make of this, Frank? I don't see how we can agree to this."

"Perhaps I should speak to Signor Conti?" Forino said. "I think I can explain to him that my associates, Messrs. Tucci and Arrigone, would show their appreciation for an assignment of Vatican business to our bank."

McHugh peered at the young man over the top of his Ben Franklin glasses, surprised at his bold suggestion. "Give it hell, Frank, but wait until I ask Conti one more question," he said.

Paul and Frank returned to Mr. Conti's office, Paul inwardly shaking with outrage at the contract demand but, as always, displaying a calm demeanor.

He said, "I must tell you that no prospective client has ever asked us for a right to approve or withhold approval of new clients. To help us evaluate the matter, are you willing to tell us what amount you spend annually on investment-banking and investment-advisory services?"

Mr. Conti smiled demurely. "I could not, of course, give you exact amounts, but I would say we spend a good deal on investment-banking fees—something on the order of thirty million US dollars last year."

This amount caused McHugh to internally and silently gasp. McHugh needed a drink of water and a moment to gather himself.

He said, "We would like to be a candidate for the position of lead financial advisor to the Holy See. You'll not find a more talented, dedicated firm in this business, nor will you find one with more worldwide institutional contacts. You need only tell me what further information you would like from us, and I will provide it. We would be honored, sir."

Forino decided to make his contribution to the conversation at that point. "Mr. Conti," he said, "I am a close associate of Enrico Tucci and Jimmy Arrigone, who greet you and ask you to give Royal Reed whatever favorable consideration you can. Mr. Tucci will particularly appreciate such a favor, as close as he has been to the Vatican."

"Ah, Mr. Tucci, he is a special friend of ours. He has helped us secure borrowing when we needed it. His Holiness is most fond of Enrico. And we are aware of Mr. Arrigone's favors to us as well. This connection changes things. It will help you greatly in securing our business."

Conti said he would be in touch, and he asked Forino to provide the personal best wishes to Messrs. Tucci and Arrigone from His Holiness, who was on a papal visit to South America and regretted his inability to host this meeting.

Signor Conti said the Vatican would conduct a confidential investigation of the business history and practices of Royal Reed and other candidates for the appointment as its investment banker, which he expected would take no more than a month. Paul told him to feel free to contact anyone in the organization, including Frank Forino or him.

Within one week, Royal Reed received a certified letter containing a form of the proposed agreement with the Vatican to appoint Royal Reed its chief investment bank and without any provision requiring Royal Reed to acquire the approval of the Vatican before becoming a financial advisor for any other client. Thus began Forino's life of great success as an investment banker.

Joe Dean

. . .

Merchandiser

• • •

Joe Dean's mother told him that it was time to move his lanky body out of the house and get a part-time job. She talked Mr. Wender at Washburn Pharmacy into paying her son a dollar an hour to do random tasks around the drugstore. He had no idea how strange those tasks could be.

Dean started out sweeping and mopping the floors in the storage room, down the aisles, and across the shoes of loitering teenagers who, in the words of Mr. Wender, were in the store only to gawk. The routine ejection of those poor souls from the store became a thing with the rhythm of the liturgy Dean had learned only too well in his altar-boy duties. He came to think in Gregorian chant of the refrain of Mr. Wender to the people he regarded as loiterers:

You're not here to buy; *ora pro nobis.*
Get your asses out of here; *orare pro nobis.*
Amen.

The only time that Dean heard Mr. Wender speak to teenage kids in a civil way was when they came to his pharmacy counter to pick up prescriptions for their parents. And even then, if they made the mistake of whispering to Wender their possible interest in something private, such as a prophylactic device or athletic supporter, his voice would ring out across the vast store through the rows of sundries to the lunch-counter patrons at the back of the store: "So you want a jockstrap, son? Is that right? What size do you want?"

One day Mr. Wender told Dean to organize the store's inventory of bandages into appropriate SKUs or shelf arrays.

"Dean," Mr. Wender said, "obviously we want to put the various types of bandages within brands and types, so all Band-Aid, 3M, Curad, and other branded bandage products go together in groups. And heavy-duty strips, wide strips, and narrow strips are separately placed. And so on. You understand? And when you're done with bandages, we'll put you on hair shampoo and other goods. We're going to modernize this place."

The notion of modernizing anything was foreign to Dean. He was offended by the idea of orderly SKUs. It struck him that marketing by displaying multiple variations of the same product was pretentious and confusing. People didn't want to have to choose among product permutations. If they needed to stop bleeding, they wanted an adhesive strip that would serve the purpose. And they did not want to deal with alternative packaging claims and come-ons. So, he devised a sort of algorithm that bollixed up Wender's whole plan by intermixing types of bandages, first with two like-branded products with similar characteristics and then with three random outliers of different brands followed by four products within a common brand that were variously packaged.

Wender examined Dean's work the next day, and a rude noise issued from the pharmacy counter to the storeroom where Dean leaned on his broom in an early stage of a daytime nap.

"Dean, come out here," shouted Wender. "What in the name of Procter & Gamble did you think I asked you to do yesterday? It's going to take me a month to straighten out the mess you've created.

Now, go back to your cleaning work. Shape up, or you'll be demoted to a fifty-cent-an-hour job. Understand?"

"Yes, sir, Mr. Wender," Dean said, as he returned to the storage room.

Washburn was, like all pharmacies, boring to the casual observer but actually a place of some beauty and nuance. Its crown jewel was its lunch and soda counter, which had a handsome linoleum countertop surrounded by ten chrome pedestal stools upholstered with a spongy material and covered with plastic in gay colors and polka dot and striped patterns. Behind the counter were, at busy times, Mavis, a slight and kindly maiden woman whom Dean judged to be about seventy years old, and, at all times, Marge, a sturdy person who looked as though she did Roller Derby on weekends and would be pleased to use her solid hips to bump to the ground any high-school brat who said, did, or looked like he might do anything improper in the store.

No kids were allowed near the lunch counter except small children who had been brought to the store by their mothers or their lonely aunts to wait while their elders ate their grilled cheese sandwiches and french fries; these youngsters were treated to an occasional sip of the delicious cement malts turned out by Mavis and Marge. When there were empty stools, the little kids liked to spin them, creating a fearsome screech, akin to nails on blackboards but higher in pitch and more penetrating. The noise brought Mr. Wender out from behind the pharmacy counter a few times each day to approach the lunch counter, identify the offending child, stop the spinning stool, and smile like an usher at the movie house who had just caught a group of kids coming in late.

Since being rebuked for his spectacular failure to organize shelves, Dean had sought a way to ingratiate himself with Mr. Wender. It occurred to him that fixing the squeaky lunch-counter stools could be the way. Wender had tried lubricants of all kinds to no avail. He had priced the idea of replacing the ball bearings in the mechanism of the spinning stool tops or replacing the stools. Both were too expensive. Dean thought that the answer might lie in a simple remedy. One morning, when he was in the store early, to mop before the crowds descended on the place, he crouched under the lunch-counter stools, and stuffed several globs of partially chewed gum up into the ridges around the stool bottoms. It hadn't occurred to him that Marge, the lunch-counter queen, might come in early to begin making coffee and laying out morning pastries. Just as he finished installing his partially chewed gum, he looked up to see her stout figure in rolled-up nylon stockings hugging her bulging thighs, a horrible sight.

"What the Christ are you doing under there, Mr. Pasty Face?" she demanded, her hands on her hips, standing on the balls of her feet in a pose that threatened that she might be readying herself to do a butt drop on his soft belly.

He rose quickly to his feet and blurted out, "Sorry, Marge, I didn't mean to scare you."

"You didn't scare me, you little pimp. I'll be talking to Mr. Wender about you. In the meantime, you keep away from the lunch counter and the floor under it," she said with a menacing sneer.

Dean scampered out from under the stools and repaired hurriedly to the storeroom, where he sat head in hand until Mr. Wender burst through the swinging door and held out his hand as if to shake Dean's sweaty palm.

"You've saved the day," said Mr. Wender, giving him a hearty handshake. "Those lunch-counter stools were driving me crazy with their squealing. Now they don't make a noise. I tried them after Marge told me you had been under there working on them. That's great. One thing, though, my boy. Marge told me you were peeking up her skirt. Now I know what's going on with the hormonal changes of someone your age, but be careful. She'll kick you, hurt you real bad."

Wender disappeared through the storeroom door and left Dean to revel in his gum-for-ball-bearings success. Maybe, he thought, he had a future in repair work.

After that, Dean's work was not confined to mopping and sweeping. Mr. Wender appointed him to do more important jobs around the store. The next Saturday, when the store was packed, Wender called him over to the pharmacy counter and told him that a stench was coming from the lunch-counter area that he could smell way up front at the pharmacy. Dean said he couldn't smell anything, but he had hay fever and a perpetually stuffy nose.

Mr. Wender said, "Well then, you're just the man for this job. Without alarming the people eating at the counter, I want you to go put on the leather gloves in the storeroom and go back behind the counter to ferret out what is causing this god-awful smell, and get it out of there."

Being nice to me, is he now? thought Dean. Maybe he will want me to do something more important for him. Either his value had actually increased in Wender's eyes because of the lunch-counter repairs or his position was too low to ask anyone else to try to do it. But the idea that Wender wanted him to don heavy leather gloves to do the job was itself uncomfortable. Was there something really terrible that he was going to have to pick up behind the lunch counter?

Now the smell was as horribly apparent to him as he assumed it had to be to everyone nearby. Half expecting to be met with a snarling badger or large rodent of some kind, he went around the side of the counter and dropped to his knees. The patrons at the counter peered over their food at Dean, who crawled back toward the sink. Mavis fled. Marge viewed him with disdain.

A hush descended over the counter area and, it seemed, the entire store. After spending a few minutes scratching around under the sink, Dean shouted out in a voice that carried like a shotgun blast throughout the pharmacy and, it seemed, well beyond into the Washburn neighborhood: "Mr. Wender, there must be a dead rat back here!"

The lunch-counter patrons bounded off their stools and retreated. Other customers in the store put down the goods they were looking at and filed out, shaking their heads.

The Pope

• • •

THE DEANS WERE THE SORT of Catholics who believed that they should give at least one child to the church to serve it as a priest or nun. In fact, after his grade school years, Joe Dean's parents suggested to him that they would be pleased to see him enter the minor seminary for his high-school training at Nazareth Hall, which was north of Saint Paul and run by the Minneapolis–Saint Paul diocese. He thought about the minor seminary for a few months and spoke to the pastor at Holy Name Parish where his family went to church. The pastor encouraged him to go into the "sem" and get on his way to qualify as a priest, which in retrospect was a preposterous idea.

But, for various reasons, Dean decided that he had a vocation to be a priest and, in fact, that he had a vocation to be the pope of the Roman Catholic Church. The only person in whom he confided his papal aspirations was his mom, who laughed and told him he should settle down and become a parish priest, and that he was about as likely to be the pope as Benito Mussolini would have been in his day. Nonetheless, Dean entered the minor seminary starry-eyed, almost breaking into tears when he thought about how high in the hierarchy he was going to be.

At Nazareth, fifty boys in the ninth-grade class entered with Dean. This was the greatest number of high-school freshmen joining in any year from that time until the high-school seminary program was shut down in the late 1970s for lack of students. The entire herd of ninth graders, along with the one hundred and fifty upperclassmen in the high-school program and the fifty young men in their first two college years of seminary training, were housed and went to school in beautiful Italianate brick buildings. The rear courtyard of the main structure was ringed with a colonnade of marble pillars. Within that enclosure was a terrazzo walkway where college freshmen and sophomores, dressed in clerical garb, strolled as they read or pretended to read from their breviaries. A wide lawn swept down to a lake in front of the campus.

In the main building, the centerpiece was an ornately carved and gilded chapel with marble floors and statuary and an exquisitely frescoed ceiling depicting in an ornate tableau the Holy Shepherd Jesus and his sheep, the members of the church. The seminarians prayed and received communion wafers at mass each morning at six thirty, and before dinner they read aloud the Office of Vespers, prayers for one of the canonical hours of the church prescribed for formal devotion, in Latin, a language no one understood in oral or written form. The resulting cacophony would today inspire the suggestion of a visit to the psychiatrist's office for all involved in the reading, but not then, not in 1962.

In addition to the two bouts of daily prayer at mass and Vespers, the curriculum of Naz, as it was called by the students, reflected an attempt at intellectual rigor. Unfortunately, a good deal of the time that could have been spent on academic courses was devoted to church things, including an overdose of theology or, as the academic bulletin revealingly called it, "religious formation," where the teachings of the church were laid out but never debated. This training involved a thorough and undifferentiated sprinkling of philosophic and religious speculation, including the fundamentals of the church's curious sex-centered notion of natural law as a religious truth that must be obeyed. Thus, "artificial contraception" was a mortal sin, condemning to hell those who used it, at least until their next confessions, when they could tell an unaware and often slumbering priest that they were heartily sorry for using rubbers to prevent pregnancies. It's hard to know the numbers, but because of the church's rule forbidding contraception as forbidden by natural law, many women who brought up to be unquestioning followers of church doctrine died, and many otherwise happy marriages failed for trying to raise families with numbers of children beyond their means to care for. And in no small measure, due to the callous lie of the proscription against artificial birth control, the earth's population has swelled beyond its means to properly sustain human life.

The sleeping arrangements at Nazareth were primitive. All fifty of the ninth graders were in one large dorm room on the upper floor, and in the night there were so many energetic moans and noises that the students' beds sounded like boats rocking on the Sea of Galilee. Boys routinely confessed to having nocturnal emissions, as the church called the phenomenon, and the confessor would invariably ask, "Was it entirely nonelective?" No one really understood the concept of election, so the incident was routinely toted up as a sin and washed away with the other confessed transgressions in exchange for a few Our Fathers and Hail Marys. The minor seminary demonstrated conclusively, if proof were needed, the vacuity of the church's series of conceits that some honor is done to the creator to ascribe to him or her authorship of concepts such as that of elective wet dreams.

Not all was bad for Dean at the seminary. He played on the freshman basketball team and, in moments when he should have been studying, he learned the game of billiards from the older boys, an art that would serve well later in his life. But the deprivations of being trapped in clerical school soon got to Dean. The crusher came two months after he started at Naz, when on Halloween night it occurred to him that in prior years he would have been out scouring the streets with his friends, scoring candy, and contriving to run into coveys of girls who were his classmates. He seldom had a chance to flirt at night, when the magic of the autumn moon fell on the rooftops and streets and when a young man's fancy turned to something he wouldn't quite understand until later. So he made up his mind on that Halloween night to give up his dream of becoming pope and to transfer to a real high school.

He called his parents the next day and said he wanted to leave Naz. Predictably, they said he had chosen the school and had to stay there for at least one year. In fact, his parents persuaded Father Elmo "Goddamn" Levaque, one of the assistant pastors at Holy Name Church, to visit Dean at Nazareth and try to talk him into staying in the sem.

The priest appeared at Nazareth on a morning at a time that allowed Dean to get out of algebra class, so he was happy about that part of the visit. A secretary ushered him into a small room near the dean of students' office, and there sat the porkpie body of Father Elmo, who constantly wore the half smile, half grimace of someone gaseous from too large a breakfast. Father did not rise to shake his hand as Dean walked in and swung shut the door. He was looking at a sheaf of papers in a manila file as a prison warden would at an inmate's parole hearing.

"Sit down, Dean," the gruff priest said. "OK, goddamn it. Listen to me. I went to some trouble helping you get into this place. As you know, your deportment record in grade school was no prize. Anyway, contrary to what you've told your parents, you're staying here. Do you understand that, goddamn it?"

"I made a mistake, Father," said Dean. "I don't have a vocation, and I don't like it here. I want to leave as soon as possible, certainly by Christmas."

"Goddamn it," shouted Father Levaque; "forget about vocations. Didn't you hear me tell you that you're staying?"

Dean had to screw up his courage to face down the little martinet who, like most priests in those days, was used to getting his way without any lip from laymen. "I'm not going back to Nazareth Hall for a second semester, Father. I'm transferring to a normal high school as soon as possible after Christmas," he said, gulping.

The diminutive cleric blanched to be spoken to this way by one of his own parish boys, a first-year minor seminarian. He sat and stared silently at Dean. But surprisingly, after lengthy hard-eyed glaring, he said. "I don't blame you, Joe, but I don't want to be quoted on that."

Levaque got up, tousled Dean's hair, and left quickly. The whole episode led to a transfer by Dean from Nazareth Hall to Cretin High School after Christmas vacation.

Twenty years later, the post–Vietnam War attitudes of the country had largely changed society's antiquated habits, such as putting high-school children into minor seminaries. The old Nazareth Hall was sold by the diocese to the Missouri Bible College. In the hands of its new owners, it became a favorite rental location for parties and weddings.

One day, on their way to play golf in northern Minnesota, Dean and two of his priest friends who had been minor seminarians in his class at Naz, Tom Bazinet and Larry Fredericks, were driving past North Saint Paul when they decided to stop by the old minor seminary campus to see what it looked like as a born-again bible school. They saw no one outside on that bright June morning. But they entered the main building, which was still fronted by a bronze door embossed with a Raphaelite depiction of angels. They went straight to the chapel that everyone who ever attended Nazareth remembered as a beautiful place on campus. They were horrified to find that the ornate marble floor of the chapel had been covered with aqua-blue indoor-outdoor carpeting. The stained-glass windows had been removed and replaced with plain glass painted with bright depictions of roses, various colored tulips, and other flowers. The oil mural behind the altar had been replaced with something that looked like an astrological chart.

"Look at this place," said Tom Bazinet. "It looks like a ballroom from some soap opera."

Just then, a pleasant-looking man approached them and held out his hand. "I'm Pastor Ron Sunquist," he said. "Can I show you around or answer any questions?"

Father Bazinet spoke first. "A couple of us went to this school on our way to the priesthood when it was Nazareth Hall. We're thinking of renting space out here for a family wedding. We understand you do wedding receptions."

Dean did not know what Tom was up to, but he sensed he was in for a show.

"Indeed we do," beamed Pastor Ron. "We can put on a wedding of almost any size."

"Like for how many guests?"

"We can accommodate as many as four hundred guests for a summer wedding," the pastor said.

"Well, that's good. We want to have a wedding in about mid-August, and we expect to have at least three hundred guests. By the way," said Larry, "do you allow alcohol to be consumed at wedding receptions here? I know you're somewhat fundamentalist, and we just weren't sure."

"Absolutely we do. We don't impose any of our beliefs on people who ask us to cater a wedding. As a matter of fact, why don't you all come back to our conference room where I can lay out the brochures for our various wedding packages and show you more about details and estimated costs?"

In the conference room, Pastor Ron loaded onto a table five large, glossy picture books that they could walk around and view. The books described events ranging from the fruit-punch reception, the bare-bones variety for a smaller group (at about five thousand dollars), up to a full-scale show that the pastor said was the Cadillac of receptions (and cost up to one hundred thousand dollars, depending on the amount of food and alcohol consumed).

"We call this the Champagne Bride wedding," said Ron. "Doves are released at the time the vows are exchanged. And, as you can see in the picture, we include a beautiful wrought iron staircase that we set up out in the rear garden, from which the bride flings her bouquet to the excited girls below." At this point, Pastor Ron was almost trilling.

Bazinet put a possessive arm around Fredericks's shoulder. He then took Pastor Ron by the elbow and ushered him a few steps away. Gazing fondly at Larry Fredericks, he said in a stage whisper, "We're really glad about your open attitude out here, Pastor Ron, and we assume you have no objection to hosting a reception for a same-sex marriage of two priests."

The joking ended with a good laugh by all except Pastor Ron, who was bewildered by the wedding plans of his fellow clerics.

Workowitz

• • •

IN HIS FIRST DECENTLY PAID summer job, at Schmidt's Brewery, Joe Dean was assigned to the racking room. He inquired about was what was done in a racking room. His new boss, Clem Kleagle, spoke to him as to a hopeless fool. "Look, kid, if you don't know what a racking room is, what are you doing working at Schmidt's?"

"Do you put people on the rack in here?" Dean asked.

"Yeah, we put pencil necks like you on the rack, wise guy. Want to see how that feels?"

Dean said he'd pass.

"OK. Let's get you started here," said Kleagle, who ended many declarations and questions with the word "here." He begged for a "little cooperation here" and asked people whether they thought they were dealing with "a nobody here."

Kleagle's discourse was routinely rhetorical. "So," he said, "we want to give every drinker our best here, right? That means that in the racking process we don't want to inject so much gas that the brew is hot, right?"

"No, I don't get it," said Dean. "You mean the beer ends up too warm and can't be cooled?"

Kleagle studied Dean's face as if looking for some sign of intelligence. "You stupid dink," he exclaimed. "I suppose you think that's funny. Well, it isn't. Too much CO_2 in the filling process and the beer wants to escape and shoot out while you're filling the barrel—or later when the barrel is tapped. You know what tapping is, don't you?"

Dean nodded his recognition.

"Of course you know tapping. That's basically all you college jerks learn at school, isn't it? How to tap beer barrels."

Dean ignored that remark and moved on. He wanted to know about the shiny, articulated metal arms that emanated from the walls and were grabbed and manipulated into the holes in the sides of the kegs by workers who stood at numbered stations.

"Is that what I'm going to be doing—filling kegs with those metal tubes?" Dean asked.

"No. You don't have the brains for that. You're going to wait until someone else fills the barrels, and then you'll be hammering a cork into the bung hole to keep the beer in."

Kleagle tried to show him how to pop the bung cork in place without breaking it.

"You see what I'm doing here?" he said.

It didn't look overly complex. Kleagle held the cork between his thumb and index finger, placed it in the empty hole on the side of the keg, and gave it one sharp rap with a rubber-headed hammer, popping it securely into the hole. He said emphatically that the key to the operation was to be sure the cork was hit squarely in the middle. Otherwise, he said, it would break, and the beer, just loaded under pressure, would shoot out of the bung like piss from a donkey.

Kleagle said, "Now try it with an empty barrel. That's what they're called, by the way. Barrels—not kegs."

It took Dean four tries before he got a cork into its hole without splitting it. Kleagle had him do it until he was successful with a few more placements and then said that he was ready for a live test. He told Dean to go over to station one with his hammer and take the place of the incumbent bung blaster for the next few barrel fillings.

Before his first swing of the hammer, a coterie of visiting executives entered the room, led by Bob Workowitz, the Schmidt's brewmaster, a position that was part manager and part artist, lending its incumbent an old-world imprimatur of taste and knowledge.

Workowitz was a big man. As he walked around the brewery in his sharkskin suit and helmet of black hair, he looked like nothing so much as a Soviet commissar examining a rocket plant. The master, as he was referred to in the brewery, ushered his visitors to a place near the first racking station. Kleagle tried to shout over the rattle and hissing of the room to warn them away from station one, where Dean stood with his hammer, and instead to guide the group to the station of an experienced hammer wielder. But they didn't hear Kleagle, and they moved to Dean's station and stopped to watch the process.

When the first barrel came down the line and was filled, Dean poised the bung between his fingers, placed it carefully in the hole, and smacked it with his hammer just off center and hard enough to make it split in two and let fly a gush of gas-borne Schmidt's beer directly into the big face and down the front of the shiny blue suit of Bob Workowitz.

The master made a noise like a whale cow: "You son of a bitch!"

Kleagle rushed to help Workowitz dry off. He wiped him down with a large chamois cloth. Others joined in the effort. They looked like a team drying a van emerging from a car wash. The master's visitors had to turn to the opposite wall to hide their reflexive outbreak of laughter.

Once having cleared his glasses of suds, Workowitz emitted a plaintiff bellow: "Stop helping me."

Then he turned ponderously toward Clem Kleagle. He thrust his sticky face into Clem's, and said, slowly pronouncing each word as if for transcription, "Kleagle, you fire that fool!"

Larry Rose

. . .

Through Rain and Sleet and Snow

. . .

During the Christmas and New Year's vacation in his first year of college, through the intervention of a friend's father, Larry Rose was hired as a holiday overload mailman for the US Postal Service. He reported for work at the Lynnhurst postal station at nine o'clock on the morning of December 15 for a mail run that was to have begun at eight thirty. He was greeted at the door by a nervous stationmaster named Anfinson, who asked if he was Lawrence M. Rose, as if the use of his middle initial were a security measure. Having established that his new man was Lawrence M. Rose, the stationmaster shook his hand and asked if he had any questions about the job. If not, he said, Rose should pull on the blue gabardine mailman uniform hanging in locker two, take the leather mailbag hanging on peg two, and quickly get himself out on the route.

Anfinson told Rose to extract the mail out of the split boxes at the corner of Logan and Forty-Eighth and the corner of Fiftieth and Thomas and to deliver between Logan and Thomas, north and south, and between Fifty-First and Lake Harriet Boulevard, east and west. He said the keys to the split boxes holding the mail were in the ring he was delivering to Larry, with a key marked red for the box at Logan and yellow for Thomas.

"Do you understand?" he asked.

"I don't have the slightest damn idea of what you're talking about. Do you have written handouts so that I know what to do?"

Mr. Anfinson was annoyed. "Did you go to the orientation class held at the downtown post office last Saturday?" he demanded to know.

"Last Saturday I was in Boston finishing my fall-quarter finals."

"And is that supposed to be my fault?"

"Just point me to my uniform and my bag," Rose said. "I'll figure it out."

"That's the boy," said Anfinson, smiling for the first time. Then his face turned serious again. "Just remember, Larry. When you step out the door of this station, you will be on federal government business delivering the US mail. Think of it as your sworn duty, because that's what it is. Keep in mind that the mail and the split-box keys you carry are official property. And be back here at four thirty sharp to return the government keys and uniform that I've entrusted to you. That's important. OK?"

Rose changed in the locker room from his street clothes to a one-piece blue uniform, donned a fur-lined hat that made him look like an outdoorsman, grabbed the mail pouch, and burst out the front door, ready to do his duty. As he emerged outside, the wind-driven snow smacked him in the face and almost drove him back against the postal station.

Rose successfully retrieved the mail from the split box at Logan Avenue. Then he started down the street, crisscrossing to drop the mail into home boxes or to leave it on porches. As he made his way, he encountered Bob Rumby, who was shoveling snow from the sidewalk in front of his parents' house.

"Rose, is that you in the mailman outfit?" Bob said, laughing with exaggerated vigor, which resulted in his slipping on the icy sidewalk and falling down in a snowbank. "Come on in, and have a morning beer with me. No one is home."

Rose explained the impossibility of stopping, given his position as a federal mail officer.

"OK. Stop back here later today when you get thirsty, and we'll have a few beers," Rumby said.

After two hours, Rose had delivered the packets held together with rubber bands and the few single envelopes of mail to the territory border at Thomas Avenue. He turned right at Thomas and started down the hill toward Lake Harriet. Halfway to Harriet, a dog barked behind him. He turned and held out his hand to the beast. The dog backed up, obdurately avoiding being petted. It was a noisy Labrador, whose heightened level of barking soon summoned two more curs to join in a group yapping at him. He faced them and took a step toward the pack. Now they leaned back on their rear legs, as domesticated dogs do when they are confronted with a foe, and bared their teeth, fixing their gimlet gazes directly on him and snarling ominously. He made a quick decision and began to run down the street. He stayed a few steps ahead of the dogs until he crossed Lake Harriet Boulevard and reached the newly frozen edge of the shore of the lake. He stepped out to a thin covering of ice near the shore. His feet poked through the early winter cover and he slipped, falling into a foot of water, the mail pouch flying. That quelled the interest of the dogs. The open top of his mailbag expelled a few loose envelopes, which slipped under the ice adjoining the spot where he lay.

He got up carefully and tiptoed onto the shore, looking about furtively in the hope that no one had witnessed his plunge. He began to trudge away from the water and back up the hill, a chill immediately settling into his bones. He couldn't stay outside in freezing wet clothes, so his decision was easy—back to Bob Rumby's house for some warmth and a beer or two. He moved up Thomas to the corner, and, looking like a person competing in a burlap-bag race at a summer picnic, he broke into a limping run until he turned on Forty-Ninth and reached Bob's house two blocks down the street.

"Ah, yes, Mr. Rose, I see you took a dip in the water," said Rumby, opening the door to let him in. "Follow me downstairs to the rec room, and we'll get you a beer and hang up your clothes to dry."

Rumby turned on the television to *Let's Make a Deal*. They draped the mailman uniform and Rose's underwear over the clothesline in the laundry room. Rose wrapped himself in an old blanket that had been hanging on the line, and Rumby opened two bottles of beer. When the show was over, they checked Rose's clothes on the line and decided they should throw them in the dryer. *The Price Is Right* was on the television, and they cracked another beer to watch it. After the show, they checked the progress of the drying. The mail-man's uniform was now a warm and sodden pile. It could barely be lifted out of the dryer. They hauled it out onto the floor, where if fell and lay like a fat squid.

"This dryer of your mother's, did she get it from the Salvation Army or what? Look at my uniform, Rumby. It is dead. What the hell am I going to do now? Could you do me a huge favor and let me use some of your dry things just to finish my route to try to get back on time? It's two o'clock now, and I'm supposed to be back at the station by four thirty."

"Sure. You can use some dry underwear and my snowmobile suit, and that way you'll really warm up. Come back after work, and we'll swap clothes."

Out again Rose went, now moving as swiftly as he could in Rumby's black Arctic Cat suit, delivering the mail parcels, some of which were soggy from the lake. He went about his work with a degree of careless haste, skipping mailboxes and throwing the mail onto porches if he heard or saw evidence of a dog. It was now three thirty, and he knew he wasn't going to finish on time. Just then, Rumby drove up and told him to get in. He said he would drive Rose door to door to deliver the remaining mail. They took off with the still-loaded mail pouch. Now Rumby crawled along the street in his car as Rose did one side of a street and got a ride back to the beginning of the street on the other side.

Rumby dropped him off at the Saint Clair post station at ten minutes after five. As he hurried through the front door, Rose beheld a shattered man—the stationmaster Anfinson.

"Jesus God, man!" Anfinson exclaimed. "Where have you been? You know you have the keys to three government split boxes." He seized the ring of keys that Rose held out to him.

"And what in the world are you wearing? I hope you did not deliver the US mail in a snowmobile suit. Where is your uniform?"

Larry Rose was too exhausted to explain. "Mr. Anfinson," he said, "I'll tell you all about it in the morning when I come in."

He hung up his mail pouch and walked out the door, leaving the boss near tears.

Gaspipe and the Creoles

· · ·

LARRY ROSE JOINED THE MUSICIAN'S union when he was a junior in college. He got occasional calls from Hector Garcia, the union rep, because Garcia knew he was in the union, and he had heard him play guitar in rock bands around town. One call would be to play country and western at the Flame Bar with a band that needed a rhythm man; the next call would be a request for him to sit in with a jazz combo at a wedding party. Several bookings were for stand-in rhythm or sometimes lead guitar in local rock bands. He needed the money and took every job he could.

One day, though, he got an odd request from Hector to sit in at the Padded Cell night club in Minneapolis for a week's run as the rhythm guitar player in the calypso or "island stylings" group known as Gaspipe and the Creoles.

"But, Hector, I don't know diddly about calypso," he said. "It's completely foreign to me."

"Listen to me, Larry. Do you know the song "Kingston Town"? Do you know "Matilda"?

"Yeah, I know those two because they were on the charts. They were Harry Belafonte songs. But that exhausts my calypso knowledge."

"I'll bet it doesn't," said Augie. "I'm sure you know the song "Yellow Bird."

"Yeah, I guess I know that one too, but that's the only other one I know in the calypso genre."

"You probably know more if you think about it. The point is, though, if you know only those three songs, so far as the drunken audience at the Padded Cell is concerned, you will be a calypso virtuoso. I'll tell you what. You call Bob Gregory at 391-3281. Bob is the Gaspipe in Gaspipe and the Creoles, and he'll set you up with whatever you need to know to play in his band. And remember a few things when you're thinking about this great opportunity. This is a booking at the Padded Cell, where Peter fucking Paul and Mary played last year! Remember, you'll be paid way above union scale. And you're just being asked to play rhythm guitar. In a calypso band, the only melody instruments are lead guitar and pipes. There's nothing to playing calypso rhythm. I could probably do it."

So Rose called Bob Gaspipe Gregory and said he had been asked to join his Creoles for a one-week gig at the Padded Cell. He said he needed work on learning calypso rhythm.

"Don't you worry about a thing, Larry. Get yourself over to my apartment on Sunday about noon. Some of the band guys will be there. We'll straighten you out. I live near the Triangle Bar on Cedar Avenue on the West Bank: 201 Cedar, apartment 505. Can you find it?

"Yeah, I can find it, but—" said Larry. He heard an abrupt click on the phone.

On Sunday, he mounted the ancient stairs to the fifth floor of 201 Cedar with his Gibson steel-string guitar. Spicy aromas filled the air all the way up. By the time he got to the third-floor landing, he could hear music filtering down from the fifth floor.

When he turned the corner to enter the fifth-floor hallway, he witnessed chaos. Three small, naked children raced toward him down the hall. Two dreadlocked men wrestled, apparently over a piece of lemon pie, which, after a miraculously long stand on its plate, flew in the air and crashed against the wall.

Rose moved along, searching for apartment 505. And there, in the doorway of 505, was Gaspipe himself, whom he recognized from pictures in the paper. He was a benign-looking island man wearing Bermuda shorts and no shirt. His chest was forested with ringlets of hair.

He smiled and held out his hand to shake. He said, "You have to be Larry, my new guitarist." Gaspipe's teeth were so framed in his dark Caribbean face that they looked fake, like Halloween chompers.

Rose followed Gaspipe into his apartment, a place of astonishing mess. The floor was littered with pillows, old food on the verge of going gray was drying on unwashed plates on every available table-top, and cats were sleeping on the furniture and preening in the arms of young bodies. One disheveled and half-dressed soul stood asleep in a corner.

"That," Gaspipe said, "is our lead guitar man, Tosh Abrams."

"What's wrong with him? He looks seriously worn out," I said.

"I wish that were all. I'm afraid he got some kind of drug poisoning this morning after a big party last night. But perhaps it is only hangover in flu's clothing. Right now, the boy's got a problem."

"I hope Tosh recovers so that he can play tomorrow for the first night of your gig," Larry said.

"That would be our gig, man. You are in the band now."

"So what happens if Tosh craps out and doesn't play tomorrow night? I hope you're not thinking that I could take his place on lead guitar. I don't know enough about calypso to be on rhythm guitar, let alone lead."

"All right, let's take care of the rhythm part right now. Follow me into the kitchen."

In the kitchen, which was cleaner than the other rooms, Gaspipe grabbed a large steel cooking pot, turned it over, and began to beat on it, at first randomly and then developing a rhythm. "Now, watch me, Larry Rose. I'm going to show you the trick to learning the basic calypso beat. See? I beat on the pan once with my right hand, once with my left, and then repeat that. After four beats, I hit it once with my right hand and twice with my left hand. Then you've got bum-bum-bum-bum-bum. Bumbum. That, right there, is the whole trick. Now you try."

Rose spent the next half hour beating on the cooking pan while Gaspipe sang songs at the top of his lungs, switching from song to song without changing the backbeat rhythm. Larry felt better when they were finished.

The next night was the start of the Creoles' gig at the Padded Cell. Larry showed up in the backstage dressing room one hour before their start time, which was eight thirty. The whole band appeared to be present and ready for action, except the lead guitarist, Tosh, who was slumped down on the floor against a wall, looking distantly into space at a vision that Rose assumed only Tosh could see. Alarmed, Rose went directly to Gaspipe's side.

"Mr. Gregory," he asked, "Tosh is going to be able to play, isn't he? I mean, I assure you that you don't want me out there as your sole guitar man."

"Assure? Forget it, Larry. You are my man," said the bandleader, smiling widely. "And, I'm not Mr. Gregory. I'm Gaspipe. OK? Do you know why they call me Gaspipe? Because when I ran track for the school right up the road in Minnesota at Saint Cloud College, I was a scared little boy from Trinidad. I was afraid I'd lose my scholarship and be sent home by the monks, so I ran so fast that I left the other runners in the fumes, like exhaust from my gas pipe. That's how it's going to be with you on that stage. You'll be nervous, but the calypso music will flow into your fingers."

The big man hugged Rose and said, "You're going to be great. And anyway, any of your sins will be covered up by the drumming and by my loud voice."

On the stage, Larry stumbled through two songs before he snapped a string on his guitar, but the din in the room was as loud as promised by Gaspipe. Larry's unpracticed calypso guitar technique, even with the broken string, did not seem to be noticed by the audience.

When the first set was concluded, Gaspipe introduced each band member. He introduced Rose as a promising folk musician and asked him to play a tune solo. Rose replaced his broken string and played and sang Bob Dylan's song, "Knockin' on Heaven's Door." That started a good part-time career for him as a solo player around Minneapolis.

No drinks or food items were thrown at the band that night or during the ensuing week's engagement. And Gaspipe Gregory said he admired Rose's courage, which Rose chose to take as a compliment.

Waite

. . .

Financial Crisis

. . .

A SUCCESSFUL FIFTEEN-YEAR PERIOD OF practicing corporate and securities litigation in Minneapolis changed Martin Waite from a young, idealistic lawyer, whose chief concern was for his clients who had been ripped off by securities dealers, to a highly paid man with a high personal overhead who worried about his security and his need to stay ahead in the game to ensure his family's ability to maintain a life that included the best private schools for his children, vacation travel, and expensive housing. In 1996, he took the position of chief risk and compliance lawyer for the major New York investment bank of G. R. Hudson Securities. He, his wife, Mary Ellen, and his two teenage sons moved to a condominium on the upper east side of New York City. The boys went to a private prep school in Manhattan. The Waites loved living in New York for its cultural and entertainment amenities and because Martin's job had high compensation and was in the exciting world of financial services. The thrill of the job started to turn into trouble, though, in the early 2000s when Hudson and the other big institutions were deregulated and allowed to do business in both commercial and investment banking, opening their ability to begin to subject customer funds to the risks of securities trading.

Before they knew it, the Waite sons were grown, had graduated from college, and were about the business of starting their own families. In 2007, Martin and Mary Ellen took a vacation in Ireland, the home of her ancestors, for a much-needed respite for him from his increasingly pressure-filled job and for her from hearing about his job troubles every night.

On the evening of the first day of their vacation, after taking an airy stroll on the streets of the Temple Bar district and combing around the beautiful grounds, lawns, and hedges of Trinity University, they returned to their room on the third floor of the Dublin Arms Hotel.

Waite opened the door and found on the threshold a typed note: "M. Waite, stay away from UK and Ireland trading or Mary Ellen will be a widow.—A Friend." He backed out of the door and showed the note to Mary Ellen. The written warning flayed his spirit like a barbed whip.

"Christ, with friends like this…" Martin said, trying to wedge out a wry smile.

"What do you suppose this is all about?" Mary Ellen said. "And how does he know my name?"

"Why do you call whoever did this 'he'?"

"Isn't that what people do: identify their enemies as 'he'?"

She took the plastic key card for the room out of her purse and moved it toward the slot to unlock their door. Martin grabbed her wrist and held back her hand before the plastic contacted the metal. "Wait, M. E.; there could be someone in there. I think we should vacate quickly without entering our room now."

"We just arrived in Ireland," she said indignantly, "so you could get away from the pressure of being forced to act as a damn government informant or spy or whatever you call it, and I'm here for the same reason: to have some fun and relax. Let's ignore this and get on with our vacation."

He checked with her to confirm that their bags were still packed and waiting inside the room. Then Waite put his arms around his wife, held her briefly, and pulled her down the hallway away from their room to the emergency exit stairwell. He opened the exit door slowly, hoping no one was waiting for them on the other side. Then, feeling weighty resistance as he pushed on it, he lowered his shoulder, crashed into the door, and heard a grunt as it contacted a body. He pushed Mary Ellen back, jumped through the door, and caught sight of a very large man lifting off the landing and tumbling down the stairs onto a lower landing.

He waited for the inevitable appearance of an accomplice. A round little man in a baseball cap appeared from a side door and stepped over his still partner, looking up the stairway directly at Martin and Mary Ellen. He reached inside his jacket, drew out a gun, and aimed it toward them.

"Don't make another move, Porky," Waite shouted loudly, pretending to reach for a gun inside his jacket pocket. The fatso fled.

He took Mary Ellen's hand and pulled her after him down two flights of stairs, stepping over the supine body of the guy he had knocked down the stairs. They went through the portal of an outside exit into an alley next to the hotel. Waite looked up and down the alley and quickly fell to one knee to aim a phantom gun at the retreating man in the baseball cap, who was now running away from them down the alley, turning to look back fearfully. The runner tripped and fell flat, doing a cement face-plant, and the Waites ran the other way, out of the alley into daylight.

Martin hailed down a black Rolls taxi, threw Mary Ellen into the back seat, and followed behind her. He waved a twenty-pound note over the driver's shoulder and said sharply, "Move quickly out of here. We have a train waiting in Kilkenny." When the cabbie delayed, Waite laid a heavy hand on the back of his neck and said in a commanding voice, "Get your ass moving. Now. Pull up around the corner and stop in front of the Dublin Arms."

The driver responded, pulling out with a lurch. As they turned out of the alley and down the street, Waite placed his hand behind Mary Ellen's head and eased her down to a kneeling position on the surprisingly well-carpeted and clean floor of the back seat of the black taxi. The Irish had ascended to the standard of the English in such matters as taxicabs at the same time they left in their frothy wake the much larger British economy. This stray thought took Waite temporarily out of the moment until the cab pulled up and stopped in front of their hotel. As he stepped out onto the street, Waite said to the driver, "I'll be back within a few minutes. I've got to grab some luggage out of our room. Now, if you're not here when I come out, or if you fail to protect my wife on the floor behind you, I'll find you fast, and you will be one sorry cabbie. Understand?"

"Yes, sir," said the driver, frightened at this threat from the big American whose wide hand he had seen over his shoulder.

Waite now saw the cabbie to be a boy, so he tousled his hair and said, "Don't worry. We'll be out of here in a minute, and you'll be safe and a little wealthier."

With that, Waite opened the cab door and strode into the Dublin Arms calmly, as if nothing was awry. He rode in the lift to the third floor, entered their room, and checked to see that everything was in their suitcases. Before he left, he tucked his few business files into the side compartment of his bag. He reappeared at the cab and threw the luggage onto the wide back cushion. When he was seated, the cab shot off, turning around the next corner and then heading over the River Liffey Bridge, toward the western-bound highway.

"How much will it be to drive us to Mount Juliet golf course in Kilkenny?" Waite asked. "And what's your name, boy?"

"I don't travel as far as Kilkenny, sir," the cabbie replied. "And my name is Emmett O'Hara."

"You'll travel that far today, Emmett," Waite said. "We have a train waiting for us in Kilkenny. And I'll pay you handsomely."

"I'll take you," said Emmett, "but there are no trains at Mount Juliet."

Waite laid a gentle paw on the back of Emmett's head. The boy's curly hair reminded him of his own son Gerald. "It's OK if there are no trains at Mount Juliet, Emmett. We like to play golf as well as ride trains. But now slow down a tad, will you? You're doing about one hundred twenty clicks an hour in an eighty zone. And you're on the wrong side of the road, boy."

They all laughed at the reference to the reversed traffic lanes in Ireland, even Mary Ellen, who was still trembling down on the floor. Waite helped her back up to the seat, threw his meaty arm around her shoulder, and kissed her full on the mouth. Emmett saw the smooch in the rear view mirror and felt more comfortable. They moved through the lengthening shadows of town into the brilliant October sunlight of the countryside. Waite took out his secure cell phone and asked to be connected to the Mount Juliet Golf and Equestrian Club.

"This is Mark Jonas," he said, using an alias to the operator at the club. "Please connect me to the proprietor, my cousin Tom Mulcahy."

"I'm sorry, Mr. Jonas, Mr. Mulcahy is traveling abroad. How may we help you?"

"My wife and I should like your best accommodations in the manor house, beginning tonight."

"Of course, Mr. Jonas. If you are Mr. Mulcahy's cousin, we will have a suite waiting for you. How long will you be staying?"

"Four or five nights, I would say," said Waite.

"When will you arrive, sir?"

"Within the hour. And so I may thank you properly when we arrive, what is your name?"

"Dierdre, sir."

"Well then, Dierdre, we'll see you presently."

As they passed through the center of Kilkenny, Emmett pointed out in the city-center square a display of the famous Kilkenny black slabs of marble commemorated in the cherished Irish folk tune "Carrickfergus."

The mile drive entering the grounds of Mount Juliet was an encounter with ancient sylvan Ireland before the English denuded a good part of the island of its native trees. They passed by a few holes on the emerald golf course, through the lot in front of the Nicholas Moss pottery shop, and, finally, to the manor house, where liveried doormen came out and helped them carry their bags from the taxicab, offering a hand to help Mary Ellen from the car.

The doorman said, "Good evening, Mr. Jonas. It is a pleasure to see you at Mount Juliet."

Waite disembarked and walked to the driver's window. Handing Emmett two hundred-pound notes, he said, "Thanks for your service, Em. Remember, though—you never saw us." Emmett smiled before briskly pulling away like a fireman from a knocked-down blaze.

"Why did you tell the driver to pretend he never saw us?" Mary Ellen asked him.

"Because, my dear, no matter how long we stay, we were never here."

Waite was not used to this regimen of ghost living, but the threat of becoming the target of government proceedings made it easy for him to adopt secrecy as a way of life. Still, it would be hard on Mary Ellen, and even on him, to resign to the reality that one really could have no absolute identity.

Back in New York, Waite leaned into the conference phone speaker to hear the Brazil office manager. "The mortgage-backed-derivatives business in Brazil is threatening to cave in," Gabriel

Allant said. "Our buyers are increasingly questioning the strength of the US housing market."

The head of worldwide trading, Sam Fargulies, replied loudly toward the speaker. "Listen, the US market is not going to recede as long as we can sell and issue well-rated, mortgage-backed bonds and the credit-default swaps that insure the pools of mortgages. It's just not going to happen."

As the chief compliance lawyer for Hudson, Waite settled back and listened to the strains of the well-rehearsed and dubiously rational recitals by the securities traders as they listed the reasons for the stability of the ever-rising mountain of mortgage-backed debt, in the issuance of which G. H. Hudson Bank played a leading role, a role Waite was scoping out from the inside of the Hudson legal department as part of negotiations with the SEC to avoid proceedings against him for the alleged aiding and abetting of the firm in selling derivative securities without accurate disclosure.

Meridel LaTrobe entered the room silently and slipped behind Waite's chair at the table where the conference call was proceeding in New York. She leaned down and intoned loudly enough for the others to hear, "Mr. Waite, L. B. Schmidt is on your office line."

Mentioning the name of this outside lawyer was her code to extract him from the weekly conference-call roundup of Hudson's foreign offices, a meeting in which he was routinely exposed to the expression of views that he couldn't afford to acknowledge without further exposing himself to potential securities-law problems. Answering legal questions thrown at him in the conference call was dangerous. It was always easier for him to respond to a request for an opinion from one of the Hudson management people by replying with his own letter, one long on assumptions, short on advice, and void of conclusions.

Outside the conference room, Meridel said to him in a confidential tone, "There is no call, but I knew you would welcome the opportunity to get out of the meeting and consider that we were just notified that the New York City Bar Association is asking you to speak at its meeting this Friday rather than next week as you have it on your calendar."

"Oh, hell, I forgot about the whole thing. But now that I think about it, this Friday works well for me. Would you just call and see what time I'm supposed to arrive? Right now, I want to be on the conference call for the Dublin portion, so I'll go back in."

When Waite returned to the meeting, the Dublin office chief was on the call and talking, as usual.

"So now, Hurley," Fargulies said, "Mr. Waite is back in the room. What did you want to ask him?"

"Hello, Martin," said Hurley. "How are you keeping yourself?"

Waite said, "Just fine, Hurls. And you?"

"We had a messy situation last week in a ritzy hotel off O'Connell Street. Two security people who are Irish boys and who have done a lot of work for us in the past got into a fracas at the Dublin Arms Hotel. One of them apparently went down a flight of stairs and ended up with a broken neck. The other got away."

"Were they working for you that day?"

"Thank God, no."

"Were the Garda called in to investigate?" asked Waite.

"Those wankers! What are they going to do of any use? But, yes. They're involved in the case, and they've been here asking questions about these two boys. The only thing they've told me so far is that their suspect made his escape in a taxi; nobody seems to have an ID on the guy."

Waite emitted a silent sigh of relief at the news that nobody knew him, but he had to hide his emotions and carry on.

"So what did you want to ask me about, Hurls?" he asked.

"I wonder whether we should have our own internal investigation of this whole incident, run out of the legal office in New York. I mean, we had nothing current going on with these two, and they were performing no services for us, but I'm worried the Hudson Bank name may get involved."

"Yes, indeed," said Waite, hoping that the name of the bank would not get involved at that point. "Because they had been used as contractors by Hudson fairly recently, we're going to be required to make a report to the SEC and the NASD—and probably to the commerce authorities in Ireland. What has been in the news so far?"

"Nothing has yet been mentioned about the security men or the culprit who got away, and the press has not connected the incident with Hudson."

"OK. Hold up answering questions until I've had a chance to think about this and to get back to you in the next few days."

After returning to New York and learning more about the investigation going on within Hudson, Waite became more concerned about the Dublin Arms incident. One night, after a worrisome day of meetings and fretting about the investigation, Waite called home.

"Hey, Mary Ellen, I have a problem. Whoever left the threatening note on our hotel-room door in Dublin may be employed by the SEC or perhaps by Hudson. Looks like I'm in the middle again."

"What are we going to do?" she asked.

"I'm afraid I do not know. Stay in the house, and don't talk to anyone today. I'll be home early."

"Early? You mean like nine o'clock?"

"I'll be home by seven o'clock."

"Yeah, right," she said, clicking off the call.

Waite slouched toward his building off Central Park East at about eight thirty that night. As he walked through the perfumed spring night air, he heard carefully planted footsteps behind him. At the next building, he backed into a recessed doorway and waited. The steps retreated in a run.

At the building where he and Mary Ellen had an apartment, he took the elevator to the twelfth floor, one above his. He descended the stairway to the eleventh floor, walked quickly down the hallway to their apartment, and let himself in with a practiced silent key turn. In the front-entrance hallway, scrawled across the light parquet wood floor were the words, "Good-bye, Mary Ellen."

He busted his way through the front, to the living room—all the while calling Mary Ellen's name—past the pictures of their two sons and one daughter, and into the master bedroom and bathroom. His eyes were drawn to furrows running through the white bedroom carpet, as if tracks from a body that had been dragged.

Waite sagged onto their big bed and thought about his poor little M. E. He walked into the hallway and looked at the recent picture of them on a California trip. She looked like a college girl with her pulled-back hairdo and her deep-blue eyes flashing in the photograph. Just then, he heard steps in the foyer and the call of his name from her unmistakable, strong voice.

"Martin, are you home?"

He bounced off the bed and bolted down the hall to the front entryway. He grabbed Mary Ellen in an exuberant hug.

"Jesus, Martin," she said. "What's gotten into you? I'm just home from the market!"

"Why does it say 'Good-bye, Mary Ellen' in lipstick on the floor in the foyer?"

"That's just erasable watercolor, not lipstick. I was just fooling around. I thought it would be a good joke about how late you are getting home from work every night."

"What are the marks across the carpet in our bedroom?"

"I don't know," she said. "Maybe from the dressing table chair I pulled across that floor to put in the hall so that I can remember to take it in for refinishing."

His face was now burning red. "Didn't I tell you to stay in the house?" he said.

"Take it easy," she said. "I was just down the block shopping for some veal."

"It doesn't matter where you go. They could grab you if they mean to do you harm."

"Who are 'they'?"

"I'm not sure who they are."

Waite couldn't be sure of much ever since the SEC started threatening him with penalties for what they theorized was his part in illegally enabling Hudson Bank in a pattern of selling mortgage-backed securities that were impossible to value and in buying hedges betting against their repayment.

"So why would someone want to do me harm?"

"I have to cooperate in snooping around and disclosing our transactions to them. Now I think my own Hudson Bank people are suspicious of me, and they might be trying to use threats against us, using security people to scare me off. That may be what was going on with people following us in Dublin. Or it may be the SEC itself, trying to cover its own incompetence or unwillingness to investigate this mortgage-bond business. I'm not sure, but I'm getting real worried."

"Let's have some dinner and get your mind off this," she said. "I'm making veal piccata and angel-hair pasta. Why don't you get out a good bottle of wine so that we can sit and talk while I putter in the kitchen?"

"Where's the cook—May?"

"Night off. Anyway, I'm sort of looking forward to cooking."

So they sat in the kitchen of their apartment—the scene of so many family gatherings and informal dinners—and talked about the grim business that faced them now. He tried to explain to Mary Ellen the complications of their problem. First, there was the question of whether the distributing and trading of real-estate mortgage-backed derivatives was being done with adequate disclosure. The US real-estate market had gotten very bubbly. Everyone knew that, including the Hudson customers who had purchased hundreds of billions of dollars in mortgage-backed bonds that now appeared to be of dubious value.

Those customers were big, sophisticated boys. Why should it be Hudson's responsibility to make sure they understood all the risks of the real-estate market? Martin wondered. Then he supplied the answer in his internal dialogue: because Hudson was the underwriter for the sale of the bonds.

In addition, he told Mary Ellen that Hudson and the other banks had pretty much bribed the rating agencies to give them AAA credit ratings on the securities that certified they were basically as riskless as bonds could be. And then the real snafu, the one that the public would be—and the authorities should be—outraged about if the mortgage market blew, was how Hudson and other banks could ethically sell those bonds and then bet against their repayment in the credit-default swap market.

Mary Ellen had tears in her eyes. She could see what a nervous wreck her husband was. She finally burst out, "The hell with this, Martin Waite. Let's pack up, go back to Minneapolis, and you can get back into the private practice of law. Let's just do it."

"It's too late. I can't get out of this now."

- End -

55079064R00082

Made in the USA
Lexington, KY
10 September 2016